I0567581

The Short Stories Of Daniel Defoe

The short story is often viewed as an inferior relation to the Novel. But it is an art in itself. To take a story and distil its essence into fewer pages while keeping character and plot rounded and driven is not an easy task. Many try and many fail.

In this series we look at short stories from many of our most accomplished writers. Miniature masterpieces with a lot to say. In this volume we examine some of the short stories of Daniel Defoe.

Daniel Defoe is most well-known for his classic novels *Robinson Crusoe* and *Moll Flanders*. Born circa 1659, he was also a journalist, a pamphleteer, a businessman, a spy ... and a writer of short stories. His life was long and colourful, and the breadth of his work, still highly regarded, is infused with similar vigor.

In these short stories, Defoe succinctly emblazons his style upon subjects as diverse as apparitions, pirates, and politics.

Defoe unfortunately often ran up large bills which could then not be repaid. He was often most seen on Sundays when bailiffs and the like legally could make no move on him. Allegedly whilst hiding from creditors he died on April 24th 1731. He was interred in Bunhill Fields, London.

These stories are also available as an audiobook from our sister company Word Of Mouth. Many samples are at our youtube channel http://www.youtube.com/user/PortablePoetry?feature=mhee The full volume can be purchased from iTunes, Amazon and other digital stores. They are read for you by Richard Mitchley & Ghizela Rowe

The Apparition Of Mrs. Veal

This thing is so rare in all its circumstances, and on so good authority, that my reading and conversation have not given me anything like it. It is fit to gratify the most ingenious and serious inquirer. Mrs. Bargrave is the person to whom Mrs. Veal appeared after her death; she is my intimate friend, and I can avouch for her reputation for these fifteen or sixteen years, on my own knowledge; and I can confirm the good character she had from her youth to the time of my acquaintance. Though, since this relation, she is calumniated by some people that are friends to the brother of Mrs. Veal who appeared, who think the relation of this appearance to be a reflection, and endeavor what they can to blast Mrs. Bargrave's reputation and to laugh the story out of countenance. But by the circumstances thereof, and the cheerful disposition of Mrs. Bargrave, notwithstanding the ill usage of a very wicked husband, there is not yet the least sign of dejection in her face; nor did I ever hear her let fall a desponding or murmuring expression; nay, not when actually under her husband's barbarity, which I have been a witness to, and several other persons of undoubted reputation.

Now you must know Mrs. Veal was a maiden gentlewoman of about thirty years of age, and for some years past had been troubled with fits, which were perceived coming on her by her going off from her discourse very abruptly to some impertinence. She was maintained by an only brother, and kept his house in Dover. She was a very pious woman, and her brother a very sober man to all appearance; but now he does all he can to null and quash the story. Mrs. Veal was intimately acquainted with Mrs. Bargrave from her childhood. Mrs. Veal's circumstances were then mean; her father did not take care of his children as he ought, so that they were exposed to hardships. And Mrs. Bargrave in those days had as unkind a father, though she wanted neither for food nor clothing; while Mrs. Veal wanted for both, insomuch that she would often say, "Mrs. Bargrave, you are not only the best, but the only friend I have in the world; and no circumstance of life shall ever dissolve my friendship." They would often condole each other's adverse fortunes, and read together Drelincourt upon Death, and other good books; and so, like two Christian friends, they comforted each other under their sorrow.

Some time after, Mr. Veal's friends got him a place in the custom-house at Dover, which occasioned Mrs. Veal, by little and little, to fall off from her intimacy with Mrs. Bargrave, though there was never any such thing as a quarrel; but an indifferency came on by degrees, till at last Mrs. Bargrave had not seen her in two years and a half, though above a twelvemonth of the time Mrs. Bargrave hath been absent from Dover, and this last half-year has been in Canterbury about two months of the time, dwelling in a house of her own.

In this house, on the eighth of September, one thousand seven hundred and five, she was sitting alone in the forenoon, thinking over her unfortunate life, and arguing herself into a due resignation to Providence, though her condition seemed hard: "And," said she, "I have been provided for hitherto, and doubt not but I shall be still, and am well satisfied that my afflictions shall end when it is most fit for me." And then took up her sewing work, which she had no sooner done but she hears a knocking at the door; she went to see who was there, and this proved to be Mrs. Veal, her old friend, who was in a riding-habit. At that moment of time the clock struck twelve at noon.

"Madam," says Mrs. Bargrave, "I am surprised to see you, you have been so long a stranger"; but told her she was glad to see her, and offered to salute her, which Mrs. Veal complied with, till their lips almost touched, and then Mrs. Veal drew her hand across her own eyes, and said, "I am not very well," and so waived it. She told Mrs. Bargrave she was going a journey, and had a great mind to see her first. "But," says Mrs. Bargrave, "how can you take a journey alone? I am amazed at it, because I know you have a fond brother." "Oh," says Mrs. Veal, "I gave my brother the slip, and came away, because I had so great a desire to see you before I took my journey." So Mrs. Bargrave went in with her into another room within the first, and Mrs. Veal sat her down in an elbow-chair, in which Mrs. Bargrave was sitting when she heard Mrs. Veal knock. "Then," says Mrs. Veal, "my dear friend, I am come to renew our old friendship again, and beg your pardon for my breach of it; and if you can forgive me, you are the best of women." "Oh," says Mrs. Bargrave, "do not mention such a thing; I have not had an uneasy thought about it." "What did you think of me?" says Mrs. Veal. Says Mrs. Bargrave, "I thought you were like the rest of the world, and that prosperity had made you forget yourself and me." Then Mrs. Veal reminded Mrs. Bargrave of the many friendly offices she did her in former days, and much of the conversation they had with each other in the times of their adversity; what books they read, and what comfort in particular they received from Drelincourt's Book of Death, which was the best, she said, on the subject ever wrote. She also mentioned Doctor Sherlock, and two Dutch books, which were translated, wrote upon death, and several others. But Drelincourt, she said, had the clearest notions of death and of the future state of any who had handled that subject. Then she asked Mrs. Bargrave whether she had Drelincourt. She said, "Yes." Says Mrs. Veal, "Fetch it." And so Mrs. Bargrave goes up-stairs and brings it down. Says Mrs. Veal, "Dear Mrs. Bargrave, if the eyes of our faith were as open as the eyes of our body, we should see numbers of angels about us for our guard. The notions we have of Heaven now are nothing like what it is, as Drelincourt says; therefore be comforted under your afflictions, and believe that the Almighty has a particular regard to you, and that your afflictions are marks of God's favor; and when they have done the business they are sent for, they shall be removed from you. And believe me, my dear friend, believe what I say to you, one minute of future happiness will infinitely reward you for all your sufferings. For I can never believe" (and claps her hand upon her knee with great earnestness, which, indeed, ran through most of her discourse) "that ever God will suffer you to spend all your days in this afflicted state. But be assured that your afflictions shall leave you, or you them, in a short time." She spake in that pathetical and heavenly manner that Mrs. Bargrave wept several times, she was so deeply affected with it.

Then Mrs. Veal mentioned Doctor Kendrick's Ascetic, at the end of which he gives an account of the lives of the primitive Christians. Their pattern she recommended to our imitation, and said, "Their conversation was not like this of our age. For now," says she, "there is nothing but vain, frothy discourse, which is far different from theirs. Theirs was to edification, and to build one another up in faith, so that they were not as we are, nor are we as they were. But," said she, "we ought to do as they did; there was a hearty friendship among them; but where is it now to be found?" Says Mrs. Bargrave, "It is hard indeed to find a true friend in these days." Says Mrs. Veal, "Mr. Norris has a fine copy of verses, called Friendship in Perfection, which I wonderfully admire. Have you seen the book?" says Mrs. Veal. "No," says Mrs. Bargrave, "but I have the verses of my own writing out." "Have you?" says Mrs. Veal; "then fetch them"; which she did from above stairs, and offered them to Mrs. Veal to read, who refused, and waived the thing, saying, "holding down her head would make it ache"; and then desiring Mrs. Bargrave to read them to her, which she did. As they were admiring Friendship, Mrs. Veal said, "Dear Mrs. Bargrave, I shall love you forever." In these verses there is twice used the word "Elysian." "Ah!" says Mrs. Veal, "these poets have such names for Heaven." She would often draw her hand across her own eyes, and say, "Mrs. Bargrave, do not you think I am mightily impaired by my fits?" "No," says Mrs. Bargrave; "I think you look as well as ever I knew you."

After this discourse, which the apparition put in much finer words than Mrs. Bargrave said she could pretend to, and as much more than she can remember - for it cannot be thought that an hour and three quarters' conversation could all be retained, though the main of it she thinks she doe; she said to Mrs. Bargrave she would have her write a letter to her brother, and tell him she would have him give rings to such and such; and that there was a purse of gold in her cabinet, and that she would have two broad pieces given to her cousin Watson.

Talking at this rate, Mrs. Bargrave thought that a fit was coming upon her, and so placed herself on a chair just before her knees, to keep her from falling to the ground, if her fits should occasion it; for the elbow-chair, she thought, would keep her from falling on either side. And to divert Mrs. Veal, as she thought, took hold of her gown-sleeve several times, and commended it. Mrs. Veal told her it was a scoured silk, and newly made up. But, for all this, Mrs. Veal persisted in her request, and told Mrs. Bargrave she must not deny her. And she would have her tell her brother all their conversation when she had the opportunity. "Dear Mrs. Veal," says Mrs. Bargrave, "this seems so impertinent that I cannot tell how to comply with it; and what a mortifying story will our conversation be to a young gentleman. Why," says Mrs. Bargrave, "it is much better, methinks, to do it yourself." "No," says Mrs. Veal; "though it seems impertinent to you now, you will see more reasons for it hereafter." Mrs. Bargrave, then, to satisfy her importunity, was going to fetch a pen and ink, but Mrs. Veal said, "Let it alone now, but do it when I am gone; but you must be sure to do it"; which was one of the last things she enjoined her at parting, and so she promised her.

Then Mrs. Veal asked for Mrs. Bargrave's daughter. She said she was not at home. "But if you have a mind to see her," says Mrs. Bargrave, "I'll send for her." "Do," says Mrs. Veal; on which she left her, and went to a neighbor's to see her; and by the time Mrs. Bargrave was returning, Mrs. Veal was got without the door in the street, in the face of the beast-market, on a Saturday (which is market-day), and stood ready to part as soon as Mrs. Bargrave came to her. She asked her why she was in such haste. She said she must be going, though perhaps she might not go her journey till Monday; and told Mrs. Bargrave she hoped she should see her again at her cousin Watson's before she went whither she was going. Then she said she would take her leave of her, and walked from Mrs. Bargrave, in her view, till a turning interrupted the sight of her, which was three-quarters after one in the afternoon.

Mrs. Veal died the seventh of September, at twelve o'clock at noon, of her fits, and had not above four hours' senses before her death, in which time she received the sacrament. The next day after Mrs. Veal's appearance, being Sunday, Mrs. Bargrave was mightily indisposed with a cold and sore throat, that she could not go out that day; but on Monday morning she sends a person to Captain Watson's to know if Mrs. Veal was there. They wondered at Mrs. Bargrave's inquiry, and sent her word she was not there, nor was expected. At this answer, Mrs. Bargrave told the maid she had certainly mistook the name or made some blunder. And though she was ill, she put on her hood and went herself to Captain Watson's, though she knew none of the family, to see if Mrs.

Veal was there or not. They said they wondered at her asking, for that she had not been in town; they were sure, if she had, she would have been there. Says Mrs. Bargrave, "I am sure she was with me on Saturday almost two hours." They said it was impossible, for they must have seen her if she had. In comes Captain Watson, while they were in dispute, and said that Mrs. Veal was certainly dead, and the escutcheons were making. This strangely surprised Mrs. Bargrave, when she sent to the person immediately who had the care of them, and found it true. Then she related the whole story to Captain Watson's family; and what gown she had on, and how striped; and that Mrs. Veal told her that it was scoured. Then Mrs. Watson cried out, "You have seen her indeed, for none knew but Mrs. Veal and myself that the gown was scoured." And Mrs. Watson owned that she described the gown exactly; "for," said she, "I helped her to make it up." This Mrs. Watson blazed all about the town, and avouched the demonstration of truth of Mrs. Bargrave's seeing Mrs. Veal's apparition. And Captain Watson carried two gentlemen immediately to Mrs. Bargrave's house to hear the relation from her own mouth. And when it spread so fast that gentlemen and persons of quality, the judicious and sceptical part of the world, flocked in upon her, it at last became such a task that she was forced to go out of the way; for they were in general extremely satisfied of the truth of the thing, and plainly saw that Mrs. Bargrave was no hypochondriac, for she always appears with such a cheerful air and pleasing mien that she has gained the favor and esteem of all the gentry, and it is thought a great favor if they can but get the relation from her own mouth. I should have told you before that Mrs. Veal told Mrs. Bargrave that her sister and brother-in-law were just come down from London to see her. Says Mrs. Bargrave, "How came you to order matters so strangely?" "It could not be helped," said Mrs. Veal. And her brother and sister did come to see her, and entered the town of Dover just as Mrs. Veal was expiring. Mrs. Bargrave asked her whether she would drink some tea. Says Mrs. Veal, "I do not care if I do; but I'll warrant you this mad fellow" meaning Mrs. Bargrave's husband "has broke all your trinkets." "But," says Mrs. Bargrave, "I'll get something to drink in for all that"; but Mrs. Veal waived it, and said, "It is no matter; let it alone"; and so it passed.

All the time I sat with Mrs. Bargrave, which was some hours, she recollected fresh sayings of Mrs. Veal. And one material thing more she told Mrs. Bargrave, that old Mr. Bretton allowed Mrs. Veal ten pounds a year, which was a secret, and unknown to Mrs. Bargrave till Mrs. Veal told her.

Mrs. Bargrave never varies in her story, which puzzles those who doubt of the truth, or are unwilling to believe it. A servant in the neighbor's yard adjoining to Mrs. Bargrave's house heard her talking to somebody an hour of the time Mrs. Veal was with her. Mrs. Bargrave went out to her next neighbor's the very moment she parted with Mrs. Veal, and told her what ravishing conversation she had had with an old friend, and told the whole of it. Drelincourt's Book of Death is, since this happened, bought up strangely. And it is to be observed that, notwithstanding all the trouble and fatigue Mrs. Bargrave has undergone upon this account, she never took the value of a farthing, nor suffered her daughter to take anything of anybody, and therefore can have no interest in telling the story.

But Mr. Veal does what he can to stifle the matter, and said he would see Mrs. Bargrave; but yet it is certain matter of fact that he has been at Captain Watson's since the death of his sister, and yet never went near Mrs. Bargrave;

and some of his friends report her to be a liar, and that she knew of Mr. Bretton's ten pounds a year. But the person who pretends to say so has the reputation to be a notorious liar among persons whom I know to be of undoubted credit. Now, Mr. Veal is more of a gentleman than to say she lies, but says a bad husband has crazed her; but she needs only present herself, and it will effectually confute that pretence. Mr. Veal says he asked his sister on her death-bed whether she had a mind to dispose of anything. And she said no. Now the things which Mrs. Veal's apparition would have disposed of were so trifling, and nothing of justice aimed at in the disposal, that the design of it appears to me to be only in order to make Mrs. Bargrave satisfy the world of the reality thereof as to what she had seen and heard, and to secure her reputation among the reasonable and understanding part of mankind. And then, again, Mr. Veal owns that there was a purse of gold; but it was not found in her cabinet, but in a comb-box. This looks improbable; for that Mrs. Watson owned that Mrs. Veal was so very careful of the key of her cabinet that she would trust nobody with it; and if so, no doubt she would not trust her gold out of it. And Mrs. Veal's often drawing her hands over her eyes, and asking Mrs. Bargrave whether her fits had not impaired her, looks to me as if she did it on purpose to remind Mrs. Bargrave of her fits, to prepare her not to think it strange that she should put her upon writing to her brother, to dispose of rings and gold, which look so much like a dying person's request; and it took accordingly with Mrs. Bargrave as the effect of her fits coming upon her, and was one of the many instances of her wonderful love to her and care of her, that she should not be affrighted, which, indeed, appears in her whole management, particularly in her coming to her in the daytime, waiving the salutation, and when she was alone; and then the manner of her parting, to prevent a second attempt to salute her.

Now, why Mr. Veal should think this relation a reflection, as it is plain he does, by his endeavoring to stifle it, I cannot imagine; because the generality believe her to be a good spirit, her discourse was so heavenly. Her two great errands were, to comfort Mrs. Bargrave in her affliction, and to ask her forgiveness for her breach of friendship, and with a pious discourse to encourage her. So that, after all, to suppose that Mrs. Bargrave could hatch such an invention as this, from Friday noon to Saturday noon, supposing that she knew of Mrs. Veal's death the very first moment, without jumbling circumstances, and without any interest, too, she must be more witty, fortunate, and wicked, too, than any indifferent person, I dare say, will allow. I asked Mrs. Bargrave several times if she was sure she felt the gown. She answered, modestly, "If my senses be to be relied on, I am sure of it." I asked her if she heard a sound when she clapped her hand upon her knee. She said she did not remember she did, but said she appeared to be as much a substance as I did who talked with her. "And I may," said she, "be as soon persuaded that your apparition is talking to me now as that I did not really see her; for I was under no manner of fear, and received her as a friend, and parted with her as such. I would not," says she, "give one farthing to make any one believe it; I have no interest in it; nothing but trouble is entailed upon me for a long time, for aught I know; and, had it not come to light by accident, it would never have been made public." But now she says she will make her own private use of it, and keep herself out of the way as much as she can; and so she has done since. She says she had a gentleman who came thirty miles to her to hear the relation; and that she had told it to a roomful of people at the time. Several particular gentlemen have had the story from Mrs. Bargrave's own mouth.

This thing has very much affected me, and I am as well satisfied as I am of the best-grounded matter of fact. And why we should dispute matter of fact, because we cannot solve things of which we can have no certain or demonstrative notions, seems strange to me; Mrs. Bargrave's authority and sincerity alone would have been undoubted in any other case.

Captain Misson

The History Of The Pyrates. Volume II. Of Captain Misson.

We can be somewhat particular in the Life of this Gentleman, because, by very great Accident, we have got into our Hands a French Manuscript, in which he himself gives a Detail of his Actions. He was born in Provence, of an ancient Family; his Father, whose true Name he conceals, was Master of a plentiful Fortune; but having a great Number of Children, our Rover had but little Hopes of other Fortune than what he could carve out for himself with his Sword. His Parents took Care to give him an Education equal to his Birth. After he had passed his Humanity and Logick, and was a tolerable Mathematician, at the Age of Fifteen he was sent to Angiers, where he was a Year learning His Exercises. His Father, at his Return home, would have put him into the Musketeers; but as he was of a roving Temper, and much affected with the Accounts he had read in Books of Travels, he chose the Sea as a Life which abounds with more Variety, and would afford him an Opportunity to gratify his Curiosity, by the Change of Countries Having made this Choice, his Father, with Letters of Recommendation, and every Thing fitting for him, sent him Voluntier on board the Victoire, commanded by Monsieur Fourbin, his Relation. He was received on Board with all possible Regard by the Captain, whose Ship was at Marseilles, and was order'd to cruise soon after Misson's Arrival. Nothing could be more agreeable to the Inclinations of our Voluntier than this Cruize, which made him acquainted with the most noted Ports of the Mediterranean, and gave him a great Insight into the practical Part of Navigation. He grew fond of this Life, and was resolved to be a compleat Sailor, which made him always one of the first on a Yard Arm, either to Hand or Reef, and very inquisitive in the different Methods of working a Ship: His Discourse was turn'd on no other Subject, and he would often get the Boatswain and Carpenter to teach him in their Cabbins the constituent Parts of a Ship's Hull, and how to rigg her, which he generously paid 'em for; and tho' he spent a great Part of his Time with these two Officers, yet he behaved himself with such Prudence that they never attempted at a Familiarity, and always paid the Respect due to his Family. The Ship being at Naples, he obtained Leave of his Captain to go to Rome, which he had a great Desire to visit. Hence we may date his Misfortunes; for, remarking the licentious Lives of the Clergy (so different from the Regularity observ'd among the French Ecclesiasticks,) the Luxury of the Papal Court, and that nothing but Hulls of Religion was to be found in the Metropolis of the Christian Church, he began to figure to himself that all Religion was no more than a Curb upon the Minds of the Weaker, which the wiser Sort yielded to, in Appearance only. These Sentiments, so disadvantageous to Religion and himself, were strongly riveted by accidentally becoming acquainted with a lewd Priest, who was, at his Arrival (by meer

Chance) his Confessor, and after that his Procurer and Companion, for he kept him Company to his Death. One Day, having an Opportunity, he told Misson, a Religious was a very good Life, where a Man had a subtle enterprising Genius, and some Friends; for such a one wou'd, in a short Time, rise to such Dignities in the Church, the Hopes of which was the Motive of all the wiser Sort, who voluntarily took upon them the sacerdotal Habit. That the ecclesiastical State was govern'd with the same Policy as were secular Principalities and Kingdoms; that what was beneficial, not what was meritorious and virtuous, would be alone regarded. That there were no more Hopes for a Man of Piety and Learning in the Patrimony of St. Peter, than in any other Monarchy, nay, rather less; for this being known to be real, that Man's rejected as a Visionary, no way fit for Employment; as one whose Scruples might prove prejudicial; for its a Maxim, that Religion and Politicks can never set up in one House. As to our Statesmen, don't imagine that the Purple makes 'em less Courtiers than are those of other Nations; they know and pursue the Reggione del Stato (a Term of Art which means Self-Interest) with as much Cunning and as little Conscience as any Secular; and are as artful where Art is required, and as barefaced and impudent when their Power is great enough to support 'em, in the oppressing the People, and aggrandizing their Families. What their Morals are, you may read in the Practice of their Lives, and their Sentiments of Religion from this Saying of a certain Cardinal, Quantum Lucrum ex ista fabula Christi! which many of 'em may say, tho' they are not so foolish. For my Part, I am quite tir'd of the Farce, and will lay hold on the first Opportunity to throw off this masquerading Habit; for, by Reason of my Age, I must act an under Part many Years; and before I can rise to share the Spoils of the People, I shall, I fear, be too old to enjoy the Sweets of Luxury; and, as I am an Enemy to Restraint, I am apprehensive I shall never act up to my Character, and carry thro' the Hypocrite with Art enough to rise to any considerable Post in the Church. My Parents did not consult my Genius, or they would have given me a Sword instead of a Pair of Beads.

Misson advised him to go with him Voluntier, and offer'd him Money to cloath him; the Priest leap'd at the Proposal, and a Letter coming to Misson from his Captain, that he was going to Leghorn, and left to him either to come to Naples, or go by Land; he chose the latter, and the Dominican, whom he furnish'd with Money, clothing himself very Cavalierly, threw off his Habit, and preceeded him two Days, staying at Pisa for Misson; from whence they went together to Leghorn, where they found the Victoire, and Signor Caraccioli, recommended by his Friend, was received on Board. Two Days after they weigh'd from hence, and after a Week's Cruize fell in with two Sally Men, the one of twenty, the other of twenty four Guns; the Victoire had but thirty mounted, though she had Ports for forty. The Engagement was long and bloody, for the Sally Man hop'd to carry the Victoire; and, on the contrary, Captain Fourbin, so far from having any Thoughts of being taken, he was resolutely bent to make Prize of his Enemies, or sink his Ship. One of the Sally Men was commanded by a Spanish Renegade, (though he had only the Title of a Lieutenant) for the Captain was a young Man who knew little of Marine Affairs.

This Ship was called the Lyon; and he attempted, more than once, to board the Victoire, but by a Shot betwixt Wind and Water, he was obliged to sheer off, and running his Guns, &c. on one Side, bring her on the careen to stop his Leak; this being done with too much Precipitation, she overset, and every Soul was lost:

His Comrade seeing this Disaster, threw out all his small sails, and endeavour'd to get off, but the Victoire wrong'd her, and oblig'd her to renew the Fight, which she did with great Obstinacy, and made Monsieur Fourbin despair of carrying her if he did not board; he made Preparations accordingly. Signior Caraccioli and Misson were the two first on board when the Command was given; but they and their Followers were beat back by the Despair of the Sally Men; the former received a Shot in his Thigh, and was carried down to the Surgeon. The Victoire laid her on board the second time, and the Sally Men defended their Decks with such Resolution, that they were cover'd with their own, and the dead Bodies of their Enemies. Misson seeing one of 'em jump down the Main-Hatch with a lighted Match, suspecting his Design, resolutely leap'd after him, and reaching him with his Sabre, laid him dead the Moment he going to set Fire to the Powder. The Victoire pouring in more Men, the Mahometans quitted the Decks, finding Resistance vain, and fled for Shelter to the Cook Room, Steerage and Cabbins, and some run between Decks. The French gave 'em Quarters, and put the Prisoners on board the Victoire, the Prize yielding nothing worth mention, except Liberty to about fifteen Christian Slaves; she was carried into and sold with the Prisoners. The Turks lost a great many Men, the French not less than 35 in boarding, for they lost very few by the great Shot, the Sally Men firing mostly at the Masts and Rigging, hoping by disabling to carry her. The limited Time of their Cruize being out, the Victoire returned to Marseilles, from whence Misson, taking his Companion, went to visit his Parents, to whom the Captain sent a very advantageous Character, both of his Courage and Conduct. He was about a Month at home when his Captain wrote to him, that his Ship was ordered to Rochelle, from whence he was to sail for the West-Indies with some Merchant Men. This was very agreeable to Misson and Signior Caraccioli, who immediately set out for Marseilles. This Town is well fortified, has four Parish Churches, and the Number of Inhabitants is computed to be about 120,0000; the Harbour is esteemed the safest in the Mediterranean, and is the common Station for the French Gallies.

Leaving this Place, they steer'd for Rochelle, where the Victoire was dock'd, the Merchant Ships not being near ready. Misson, who did not Care to pass so long a Time in Idleness, proposed to his Comrade the taking a Cruize on board the Triumph, who was going into the English Channel; the Italian readily contented to it.

Between the Isle of Guernsey and the Start Point they met with the Mayflower, Captain Balladine Commanded, a Merchant Ship of 18 Guns, richly laden, and coming from Jamaica. The Captain of the English made a gallant resistance, and fought his Ship so long, that the French could not carry her into Harbour, wherefore they took the Money, and what was most valuable, out of her; and finding she made more Water than the Pumps could free, quitted, and saw her go down in less than four Hours after. Monsieur le Blanc, the French Captain, received Captain Balladine very civilly, and would not suffer either him or his Men to be stripp'd, saying, None but Cowards ought be treated after that Manner; that brave Men ought to treat such, though their Enemies, as Brothers; and that to use a gallant Man (who does his Duty) ill, speaks a Revenge which cannot proceed but from a Coward Soul. He order'd that the Prisoners should leave their Chests; and when some of his Men seem'd to mutter, he bid 'em remember the Grandeur of the Monarch they serv'd; that they were neither Pyrates nor Privateers; and, as brave Men, they ought to shew their Enemies an

Example they would willingly have follow'd, and use their Prisoners as they wish'd to be us'd.

They running up the English Channel as high as Beachy Head, and, in returning, fell in with three fifty Gun Ships, which gave Chace to the Triumph; but as she was an excellent Sailor, she run 'em out of Sight in seven Glasses, and made the best of her Way for the Lands-End they here cruized eight Days, then doubling Cape Cornwall, ran up the Bristol Channel, near as far as Nash Point, and intercepted a small Ship from Barbadoes, and stretching away to the Northward, gave Chase to a Ship they saw in the Evening, but lost her in the Night. The Triumph stood then towards Milford and spying a Sail, endeavour'd to cut her off the Land, but found it impossible; for she got into the Haven, though they came up with her very fast, and she had surely been taken, had the Chase had been any thing longer.

Captain Balladine, who took the Glass, said it was the Port Royal, a Bristol Ship which left Jamaica in Company with him and the Charles. They now return'd to their own Coast, and sold their Prize at Brest, where, at his Desire, they left Captain Balladine, and Monsieur le Blanc made him a Present of Purse with 40 Louis's for his Support; his Crew were also left here.

At the Entrance into this Harbour the Triumph struck upon a Rock, but receiv'd no Damage: This Entrance, called Genlet, is very dangerous on Account of the Number of Rocks which lie on each Side under Water, though the Harbour is certainly the best in France. The Mouth of the Harbour is defended by a strong Castle; the Town is well fortified, and has a Citadel for its farther Defence, which is of considerable Strength. In 1694 the English attempted a Descent, but did not find their Market, for they were beat off with the Loss of their General, and a great many Men. From hence the Triumph return'd to Rochel, and in a Month after our Voluntiers, who went on board the Victoire, took their Departure for Martineco and Guadalupe; they met with nothing in their Voyage thither worth noting.

I shall only observe, that Signior Caraccioli, who was as ambitious as he was irreligious, had, by this Time, made a perfect Deist of Misson, and thereby convinc'd him, that all Religion was no other than human Policy, and shew'd him that the Law of Moses was no more than what were necessary, as well for the Preservation as the Governing of the People; for Instance, said he, the African Negroes never heard of the Institution of Circumcision, which is said to be the Sign of the Covenant made between God and this People, and yet they circumcise their Children; doubtless for the same Reason the Jews and other Nations do, who inhabit the Southern Climes, the Prepuce consolidating the perspired Matter, which is of a fatal Consequence. In short, he ran through all the Ceremonies of the Jewish, Christian and Mahometan Religion, and convinced him these were, as might be observed by the Absurdity of many, far from being Indications of Men inspired; and that Moses, in his Account of the Creation, was guilty of known Blunders; and the Miracles, both in the New and Old Testament, inconsistent with Reason. That God had given us this Blessing, to make Use of for our present and future Happiness, and whatever was contrary to it, notwithstanding their School Distinctions of contrary and above Reason, must be false. This Reason teaches us, that there is a first Cause of all Things, an Ens

Entium, which we call God, and our Reason will also suggest, that he must be eternal, and, as the Author of every Thing perfect, he must be infinitely perfect.

If so, he can be subject to no Passions, and neither loves nor hates; he must be ever the fame, and cannot rashly do to Day what he shall repent to Morrow. He must be perfectly happy, consequently nothing can add to an eternal State of Tranquillity, and though it becomes us to adore him, yet can our Adorations neither augment, nor our Sins take from this Happiness.

But his Arguments on this Head are too long, and too dangerous to translate; and as they are work'd up with great Subtlety, they may be pernicious to weak Men, who cannot discover their Fallacy; or, who finding 'em agreeable to their Inclinations, and would be glad to shake off the Yoke of the Christian Religion, which galls and curbs their Passions, would not give themselves the Trouble to examine them to the Bottom, but give into what pleases, glad of finding some Excuse to their Consciences. Though as his Opinion of a future State has nothing in it which impugns the Christian Religion, I shall set it down in few Words.

That reasoning Faculty, says he, which we perceive within us, we call the Soul, but what that Soul is, is unknown to us. It may die with the Body, or it may survive. I am of Opinion its immortal; but to say that this Opinion is the Dictate of Reason, or only the Prejudice of Education, would, I own, puzzle me. If it is immortal, it must be an Emanation from the Divine Being, and consequently at its being separated from the Body, will return to its first Principle, if not contaminated. Now, my Reason tells me, if it is estranged from its first Principle, which is the Deity, all the Hells of Man's Invention can never yield Tortures adequate to such a Banishment.

As he had privately held these Discourses among the Crew, he had gained a Number of Proselytes, who look'd upon him as a new Prophet risen up to reform the Abuses in Religion; and a great Number being Rochellers, and, as yet, tainted with Calvinism, his Doctrine was the more readily embrac'd. When he had experienced the Effects of his religious Arguments, he fell upon Government, and shew'd, that every Man was born free, and had as much Right to what would support him, as to the Air he respired. A contrary Way of arguing would be accusing the Deity with Cruelty and Injustice, for he brought into the World no Man to pass a Life of Penury, and to miserably want a necessary Support; that the vast Difference between Man and Man, the one wallowing in Luxury, and the other in the most pinching Necessity, was owing only to Avarice and Ambition on the one Hand, and a pusillanimous Subjection on the other; that at first no other than a Natural was known, a paternal Government, every Father was the Head, the Prince and Monarch of his Family, and Obedience to such was both just and easy, for a Father had a compassionate Tenderness for his Children; but Ambition creeping in by Degrees, the stronger Family set upon and enslaved the Weaker; and this additional Strength over-run a third, by every Conquest gathering Force to make others, and this was the first Foundation of Monarchy. Pride encreasing with Power, Man usurped the Prerogative of God, over his Creatures, that of depriving them of Life, which was a Privilege no one had over his own; for as he did not come into the World by his own Election, he ought to stay the determined Time of his Creator: That indeed, Death given in War, was by the Law of Nature allowable, because it is for the Preservation of our own Lives; but no Crime ought to be thus punished, nor indeed any War undertaken, but in Defence of our natural Right, which is such a Share of Earth as is necessary for our Support.

These Topicks he often declaimed on, and very often advised with Misson about the setting up for themselves; he was as ambitious as the other, and as resolute. Caraccioli and Misson were by this expert Mariners, and very capable of managing a Ship: Caraccioli had founded a great many of the Men on this Subject, and found them very inclineable to listen to him. An Accident happen'd which gave Caraccioli a fair Opportunity to put his Designs in Execution, and he laid Hold of it; they went off Martinico on a Cruize, and met with the Winchelsea, an English Man of War of 40 Guns, commanded by Captain Jones; they made for each other, and a very smart Engagement followed, the first Broadside killed the Captain, second Captain, and the three Lieutenants, on Board the Victoire and left only the Master, who would have struck, but Misson took up the Sword, order'd Caraccioli to act as Lieutenant, and encouraging the Men fought the Ship six Glasses, when by some Accident, the Winchelsea blew up, and not a Man was saved but Lieutenant Franklin, whom the French Boats took up, and he died in two Days. None ever knew before this Manuscript fell into my Hands how the Winchelsea was lost; for her Head being driven ashore at Antegoa, and a great Storm having happend a few Days before her Head was found, it was concluded, that she founder'd in that Storm. After this Engagement, Caraccioli came to Misson and saluted him Captain, and desired to know if he would chuse a momentary or a lasting Command, that he must now determine, for at his Return to Martinico it would be too late; and he might depend upon the Ship he fought and saved being given to another, and they would think him well rewarded if made a Lieutenant, which Piece of Justice he doubted: That he had his Fortune in his Hands, which he might either keep or let go; if he made Choice of the latter, he must never again expect she would court him to accept her Favours: That he ought to let before his Eyes his Circumstances, as a younger Brother of a good Family, but nothing to support his Character; and the many Years he must serve at the Expence of his Blood before he could make any Figure in the World; and consider the wide Difference between the commanding and being commanded: That he might with the Ship he had under Foot, and the brave Fellows under Command, bid Defiance to the Power of Europe, enjoy every Thing he wish'd, reign Sovereign of the Southern Seas, and lawfully make War on all the World, since it would deprive him of that Liberty to which he had a Right by the Laws of Nature: That he might in Time, become as great as Alexander was to the Persians; and by encreasing his Forces by his Captures, he would every Day strengthen the Justice of his Cause, for who has Power is always in the Right. That Harry the Fourth and Harry the Seventh, attempted and succeeded in their Enterprizes on the Crown of England, yet their Forces did not equal his. Mahomet with a few Camel Drivers, founded the Ottoman Empire and Darius, with no more than six or seven Companions got Possession on of that of Persia.

In a Word he said so much that Misson resolved to follow his Advice, and calling up all Hands, he told them, 'That a great Number of them had resolved with him upon a Life of Liberty, and had done him the Honour to create him Chief: That he designed to force no Man, and be guilty of that Injustice he blamed in others; therefore, if any were averse to the following his Fortune, which he promised should be the same to all, he desired they would declare themselves, and he would set them ashore, whence they might return with Conveniency;' having made an End, they one and all cryed, Vive le Capitain Misson et son Lieutenant le Seavant Caraccioli, God bless Capt. Misson and his learned Lieutenant Caraccioli. Misson thanked them for the Honour they conferr'd upon him, and promised he would use the Power they gave for the publick Good only, and hoped, as they had the Bravery to assert their Liberty, they would be as unanimous in the preserving it, and stand by him in what should be found expedient for the Good of all; that he was their Friend and Companion, and should never exert his Power, or think himself other than their Comrade, but when the Necessity of Affairs should oblige him.

They shouted a second Time, vive le Capitain; he, after this, desired they would chuse their subaltern Officers, and give them Power to consult and conclude upon what might be for the common Interest, and bind themselves down by an Oath to agree to what such Officers and he should determine: This they readily gave into. The School-Master they chose for second Lieutenant, Jean Besace they nominated for third, and the Boatswain, and a Quarter-Master, named Matthieu le Tondu, with the Gunner, they desired might be their Representatives in Council.

The Choice was approved, and that every Thing might pass methodically, and with general Approbation, they were called into the great Cabbin, and the Question put, what Course they should steer? The Captain proposed the Spanish Coast as the most probable to afford them rich Prizes: This was agreed upon by all. The Boatswain then asked what Colours they should fight under, and advised Black as most terrifying; but Caraccioli objected, that they were no Pyrates, but Men who were resolved to assert that Liberty which God and Nature gave them, and own no Subjection to any, farther than was for the common Good of all: That indeed, Obedience to Governors was necessary, when they knew and acted up to the Duty of their Function; were vigilant Guardians of the Peoples Rights and Liberties; saw that Justice was equally distributed; were Barriers against the Rich and Powerful, when they attempted to oppress the Weaker; when they suffered none of the one Hand to grow immensely rich, either by his own or his Ancestors Encroachments; nor on the other, any to be wretchedly miserable, either by falling into the Hands of Villains, unmerciful Creditors, or other Misfortunes. While he had Eyes impartial, and allowed nothing but Merit to distinguish between Man and Man; and instead of being a Burthen to the People by his luxurious life, he was by his Care for, and Protection of them, a real Father, and in every Thing acted with the equal and impartial Justice of a Parent: But when a Governor, who is the Minister of the People, thinks himself rais'd to this Dignity, that he may spend his Days in Pomp and Luxury, looking upon his Subjects as so many Slaves, created for his Use and Pleasure, and therefore leaves them and their Affairs to the immeasurable Avarice and Tyranny of some one whom he has chosen for his Favourite, when nothing but Oppression, Poverty, and all the Miseries of Life flow from such an Administration; that he lavishes away the Lives and Fortunes of the People, either to gratify his Ambition, or to support the Cause of some neighbouring Prince, that he may in Return, strengthen his Hands should his People exert themselves in Defence of their native Rights; or should he run into unnecessary Wars, by the rash and thoughtless Councils of his Favourite, and not able to make Head against the Enemy he has rashly or wantonly brought upon his Hands, and buy a Peace (which is the present Case of France, as every one knows, by supporting King James, and afterwards proclaiming his Son) and drain the Subject; should the

Peoples Trade be wilfully neglected, for private Interests, and while their Ships of War lie idle in their Harbours, suffer their Vessels to be taken; and the Enemy not only intercepts all Commerce, but insults their Coasts: It speaks a generous and great Soul to shake off the Yoak; and if we cannot redress our Wrongs, withdraw from sharing the Miseries which meaner Spirits submit to, and scorn to yield to the Tyranny. Such Men are we, and, if the World, as Experience may convince us it will, makes War upon us, the Law of Nature empowers us not only to be on the defensive, but also on the offensive Part. As we then do not proceed upon the same Ground with Pyrates, who are Men of dissolute Lives and no Principles, let us scorn to take their Colours: Ours is a brave, a just, an innocent, and a noble Cause; the Cause of Liberty. I therefore advise a white Ensign, with Liberty painted in the Fly, and if you like the Motto, a Deo a Libertate, for God and Liberty, as an Emblem of our Uprightness and Resolution.

The Cabbin Door was left open, and the Bulk Head which was of Canvas rowled up, the Steerage being full of Men, who lent an attentive Ear, they cried, Liberty, Liberty; we are free Men: Vive the brave Captain Misson and the noble Lieutenant Caraccioli. This short Council breaking up, every Thing belonging to the deceased Captain, and the other Officers, and Men lost in the Engagement, was brought upon Deck and over-hawled; the Money ordered to be put into a Chest, and the Carpenter to clap on a Padlock for, and give a Key to, every one of the Council: Misson telling them, all should be in common, and the particular Avarice of no one should defraud the Publick.

When the Plate Monsieur Fourbin had, was going to the Chest, the Men unanimously cried out avast, keep that out for the Captain's Use, as a Present from his Officers and Fore-mast Men. Misson thanked them, the Plate was returned to the great Cabbin, and the Chest secured according to Orders: Misson then ordered his Lieutenants and other Officers to examine who among the Men, were in most Want of Cloaths, and to distribute those of the dead Men impartially, which was done with a general Content and Applause of the whole Crew: All but the wounded being upon Deck. Misson from the Baracade, spoke to the following Purpose, 'That since they had unanimously resolved to seize upon and defend their Liberty, which ambitious Men had usurped, and that this could not be esteemed by impartial Judges other than a just and brave Resolution, he was under an Obligation to recommend to them a brotherly Love to each other; the Banishment of all private Piques and Grudges, and a swift Agreement and Harmony among themselves: That in throwing off the Yoak of Tyranny of which the Action spoke an Abhorrence, he hoped none would follow the Example of Tyrants, and turn his Back upon Justice; for when Equity was trodden under Foot, Misery, Confusion, and mutual Distrust naturally followed.'He also advised them to remember there was a Supream; the Adoration of which, Reason and Gratitude prompted us, and our own Interests would engage us (as it is best to be of the surest Side, and after-Life was allowed possible) to conciliate. That he was satisfied Men who were born and bred in Slavery, by which their Spirits were broke, and were incapable of so generous a Way of thinking, who, ignorant of their Birth-Right, and the Sweets of Liberty, dance to the Musick of their Chains, which was, indeed, the greater Part of the Inhabitants of the Globe, would brand this generous Crew with the insidious Name of Pyrates, and think it meritorious, to be instrumental in their Destruction. Self-Preservation therefore, and not a cruel Disposition, obliged him to declare War against all such as should refuse him the Entry of their Ports, and against all, who should not immediately surrender and give up what their Necessities required; but in a more particular Manner against all European Ships and Vessels, as concluded implacable Enemies. And I do now, said he, declare such War, and, at the same time, recommend to you my Comrades a humane and generous Behaviour towards your Prisoners; which will appear by so much more the Effects of a noble Soul, as we are satisfied we should not meet the same Treatment should our ill Fortune, or more properly our Disunion, or want of Courage, give us up to their Mercy.

After this, he required a Muster should be made, and there were able Hands two Hundred, and thirty five sick and wounded; as they were muster'd they were sworn. After Affairs were thus settled, they shaped their Course the Spanish West-Indies, but resolved, in the Way, to take a Week or ten Days Cruize in the Windward Passage from Jamaica, because most Merchant Men, which were good Sailors and did not slay for Convoy, took this as the shorter Cut for England.

Off St. Christophers they took an English Sloop becalmed, with their Boats; they took out of her a couple of Puncheons of Rum, and half a dozen Hogsheads of Sugar (she was a New England Sloop, bound for Boston) and without offering the least Violence to the Men, or stripping them, they let her go. The Master of the Sloop was Thomas Butler, who owned, he never met with so candid an Enemy as the French Man of War, which took him the Day he left St. Christophers; they met with no other Booty in their Way, till they came upon their Station, when after three Days, they saw a Sloop which had the Impudence to give them Chace; Captain Misson asked what could be the Meaning that the Sloop stood for them? One of the Men, who was acquainted with the West-Indies, told him, it was a Jamaica Privateer, and he should not wonder, if he clapp'd him aboard. I am, said he, no Stranger to their Way of working, and this despicable Fellow, as those who don't know a Jamaica Privateer may think him, it is ten to one will give you some Trouble. It now grows towards Evening, and you'll find as soon as he has discovered your Force, he'll keep out of the Reach of your Guns till the 12 a-Clock Watch is changed at Night, and he'll then attempt to clap you aboard, with Hopes to carry you in the Hurry: Wherefore Captain, if you will give me Leave to advise you, let every Man have his small Arms; and at twelve, let the Bell ring as usual; and rather more Noise than ordinary be made, as if the one Watch was turning in, and the other out, in a Confusion and Hurry, and I'll engage he will venture to enter his Men. The Fellow's Advice was approved and resolved upon, and the Sloop work'd, as he said she would, for upon coming near enough to make distinctly the Force of the Victoire, on her throwing out French Colours, she, the Sloop, clapp'd upon a Wind, the Victoire gave Chace, but without Hopes of gaining upon her; she went so well to Windward, that she cou'd spare the Ship some Points in her Sheet, and yet wrong her: At Dusk of the Even, the French had lost Sight of her, but about Eleven at Night, they saw her hankering up their Windward Bow, which confirmed the Sailors Opinion, that she would attempt to board them, as she did at the pretended Change of the Watch; there being little or no Wind, she lashed to the Bow-Sprit of the Victoire and enter'd her Men, who were very quietly taken, as they enter'd and tumbled down the Forehatch, where they were received by others, and bound without Noise, not one of the Privateers killed, few hurt, and only one Frenchman wounded. The Victoire the better Part of the Sloop's Men secured, they boarded in their Turn, when the Privateer's suspecting some Stratagem, were endeavouring to cut their Lashing and get off:

Thus the Englishman caught a Tartar. The Prisoners being all secured, the Captain charged his Men not to discover, thro' a Desire of augmenting their Number, the Account they were upon.

The next Morning Monsieur Misson called for the Captain of the Privateer, he told him, he could not but allow him a brave Fellow, to venture upon a Ship of his Countenance, and for that Reason he should meet Treatment which Men of his Profession seldom afforded the Prisoners they made. He asked him how long he had been out, what was his Name, and what he had on Board? He answered he was but just come out, that he was the first Sail he had met with, and should have thought himself altogether as lucky not to have spoke with him' that his Name was Harry Ramsey, and what he had on Board were Rags, Powder, Ball, and some few half Anchors of Rum. Ramsey was ordered into the Gun-Room, and a Council being held in the publick Manner aforesaid, the Bulk Head of the great Cabbin rowled up. On their Conclusion, the Captain of the Privateer was called in again, when Captain Misson told him, he would return him his Sloop, and restore him and his Men to their Liberty, without stripping or plundering of any Thing, but what Prudence obliged him to, their Ammunition and Small-Arms, if he would give him his Word and Honour, and his Men to take an Oath, not to go out on the Privateer Account in six Months after they left him: That he did not design to continue that Station above a Week longer, at the Expiration of which Time he would let them go.

Ramsey, who had a new Sloop, did not expect this Favour, which he thanked him for, and promised punctually to comply with the Injunction, which his Men as readily swore to, tho' they had no Design to keep the Oath. The Time being expired, he and his Men were put on Board their own Sloop. At going over the Ship's Side Ramsey begg'd Monsieur Misson would allow him Powder for a salute, by way of Thanks; but he answered him, the Ceremony was needless, and he expected no other Return than that of keeping his Word, which indeed Ramsey did. Some of his Men had found it more to their Advantage to have been as religious.

At parting Ramsey gave the Ship three Chears, and Misson had the Complaisance to return one, which Ramsey answering with three more, made the best of his Way for Jamaica, and at the East End of the Island met with the Diana, who, upon Advice, turn'd back.

The Victoire steer'd for Carthagene, off which Port they cruised some Days, but meeting with nothing in the Seas, they made for Porto Bello; in their Way they met with two Dutch Traders, who had Letters of Mart, and were just come upon the Coast, the one had 20, the other 24 Guns; Misson engaged them, and they defended themselves with a great Deal of Resolution and Gallantry; and as they were mann'd a Peak, he darst not venture to board either of them, for fear of being at the same Time boarded by the other. His Weight of Mettal gave him a great Advantage over the Dutch, though they were two to one; besides, their Business, as they had Cargoes, was to get off, if possible, wherefore they made a running Fight, though they took Care to stick close to one another.

They maintained the Fight for above six Hours, when Misson, enraged at this Obstinacy, and fearing, if by Accident they should bring a Mast, or Top-Mast, by the board, they would get from him. He was resolved to sink the larger Ship of the two, and accordingly ordered his Men to bring all their Guns to bear a Midship, then running close along Side of him, to raise their Mettal; his Orders being punctually obey'd, he pour'd in a Broad Side, which open'd such a Gap in the Dutch Ship, that she went directly to the Bottom, and every Man perish'd.

He then mann'd his Bowsprit, brought his Sprit-sail Yard fore and aft, and resolved to board the other, which the Dutch perceiving, and terrified with the unhappy Fate of their Comrade, thought a farther Resistance vain, and immediately struck. Misson gave them good Quarters, though he was enraged at the Loss of 13 Men killed outright, beside 9 wounded, of which 6 died. They found on board a great Quantity of Gold and Silver Lace, brocade Silks, Silk Stockings, Bails of Broad- Cloath, bazes of all Colours, and Osnabrughs.

A Consultation being held, it was resolved Captain Misson should take the Name of Fourbin, and returning to Carthagene, dispose of his Prize, and set his Prisoners ashoar. Accordingly they ply'd to the Eastward, and came to an Anchor between Boca Chieca Fort, and the Town, for they did not think it expedient to enter the Harbour. The Barge was manned, and Caraccioli, with the Name of D'Aubigny, the first lieutenant, who was killed in the Engagement with the Winchelsea, and his Commission in his Pocket, went ashore with a Letter to the Governor, sign'd Fourbin, whose Character, for fear of the worst, was exactly counterfeited. The Purport of his Letter was, that having discretionary Orders to cruize for three Months, and hearing the English infested his Coast, he was come in search of 'em, and had met two Dutch Men, one of which he had sunk, the other he made Prize of. That his limited Time being near expired, he should be obliged to his Excellency, if he would send on board him such Merchants as were willing to take the Ship and Cargoe off his Hands, of which he had lent the Dutch Invoice. Don Joseph de la Zerda, the then Governor, received the Lieutenant (who sent back the Barge at landing) very civilly, and agreed to take the Prisoners ashoar, and do every Thing was required of him; and ordering fresh Provisions and Sallading to be got ready as a Present for the Captain, he sent for some Merchants who were very ready to go on board, and agree for the Ship and Goods; which they did, for two and fifty thousand Pieces of Eight. The next Day the Prisoners were set ashoar; a rich Piece of Brocade which was reserv'd, sent to the Governor for a Present, a Quantity of fresh Provision bought and brought on board, the Money paid by the Merchants, the Ship and Goods deliver'd, and the Victoire, at the Dawn of the following Day, got under Sail. It may be wonder'd how such Dispatch could be made, but the Reader must take Notice, these Goods were sold by the Dutch Invoice, which the Merchant of the Prize affirmed was genuine. I shall observe, by the by, that the Victoire was the French Man of War which Admiral Wager sent the Kingston in search of, and being afterwards falsly inform'd, that she was join'd by another of seventy Guns; and that they cruiz'd together between the Capes, order'd the Severn up to Windward, to assist the Kingston, which had like to have prov'd very fatal; for these two English Men of War, commanded by Captain Trevor and Captain Padnor, meeting in the Night, had prepared to engage, each taking the other for the Enemy. The Kingston's Men not having a good Look-out, which must be attributed to the Negligence of the Officer of the Watch, did not see the Severn till she was just upon them; but, by good Luck, to Leeward, and plying up, with all the Sail she could crowd, and a clear Ship. This put the Kingston in such Confusion, that when the Severn hal'd, no answer was retun'd, for none heard her. She was got under the Kingston's Stern, and Captain Padnor ordered to hale for the third and last Time, and if no answer was return'd, to give her a Broadside. The Noise onboard the Kingston was now a little ceas'd, and Captain Trevor, who was on the poop with a speaking Trumpet to hale the Severn, by good Luck heard her hale him, answering the Kingston, and asking the Name of the other ship, prevented the Damage.

They cruised together some time, and meeting nothing which answer'd their Information, return'd to Jamaica, as I shall to my Subject, begging Pardon for this, as I thought, necessary Digression.

Don Juan de la Zevda told the Captain in a Letter, that the St. Joseph, a Gallion of seventy Guns, was then lying at Port a Bello, and should be glad he could keep her Company till she was off the Coast. That she would sail in eight or ten Days for the Havana; and that, if his Time would permit him, he would send an Advice-Boat. That she had on board the Value of 800,000 Pieces of Eight in Silver and Bar Gold. Misson return'd Answer, that he believ'd he should be excus'd if he stretched his Orders, for a few Days; and that he would cruize off the Isle of Pearls, and Cape Gratias a Dios, and give for Signal to the Gallion, his spreading a white Ensign in his Fore-Top-Mast Shrouds, the cluing up his Fore-sail, and the firing one Gun to Windward, and two to Leeward, which he should answer by letting run and hoisting his Fore- Top-Sail three times, and the firing as many Guns to Leeward. Don Joseph, extreamly pleased with this Complaisance, sent a Boat express to advise the St. Joseph, but she was already sailed two Days, contrary to the Governor of Carthagene's Expectation, and, this Advice Captain Misson had from the Boat, which returning with an Answer, saw the Victoire in the Offin, and spoke to her. It was then resolved to follow the St. Joseph, and accordingly they steer'd for the Havanna, but by what Accident they did not overtake her is unknown.

I forgot to tell my Reader, on Board the Dutch Ship were fourteen French Hugonots, whom Misson thought fit to detain, when they were at Sea. Misson called 'em up, and proposed to 'em their taking on; telling them at the same Time, he left it to their Choice, for he would have no forc'd Men; and that if they all, or any of them, disapproved the Proposal, he would either give 'em the first Vessel he met that was fit for 'em, or set 'em ashoar on some inhabited Coast; and therefore bid 'em take two Days for Consideration before they returned an Answer; and, to encourage 'em, he called all Hands up, and declar'd, that if any Man repented him of the Course of Life he had chosen, his just Dividend should be counted to him, and he would set him on Shoar, either near the Havanna, or some other convenient Place; but not one accepted the Offer, and the fourteen Prisoners unanimously resolved to join in with 'em; to which Resolution, no doubt, the Hopes of a good Booty from the St. Joseph, and this Offer of Liberty greatly contributed.

At the Entrance of the Gulph they spied and came with a large Merchant Ship bound for London from Jamaica; she had 20 Guns, but no more than 32 Hands, that its not to be wonder'd at she made no Resistance, besides, she was deep laden with Sugars. Monsieur Misson took out of her what Ammunition she had, about four thousand Pieces of Eight, some Puncheons of Rum, and ten Hogsheads of Sugar; and, without doing her any further Damage, let her proceed her Voyage. What he valued most in this Prize was the Men he got, for she was carrying to Europe twelve French Prisoners, two of which were necessary Hands, being a Carpenter and his Mate. They were of Bourdeaux, from whence they came with the Pomechatraine, which was taken by the Maremaid off Petit Guavers, after an obstinate Resistance, in which they lost forty Men; but they were of Opinion the Maremaid could not have taken 'em, having but four Guns less than she had, which was made amends for, by their having about thirty Hands. On the contrary, had not the Guernsey come up, they thought of boarding and carrying the Maremaid. These Men very willingly came into Captain Misson's Measures.

These Men, who had been stripp'd to the Skin, begg'd Leave to make Reprisals, but the Captain would not suffer them, though he told the Master of the Prize, as he protected him and his Men, he thought it reasonable these French should be cloathed: Upon this the Master contributed of his own, and every Man bringing up his Chest, thought themselves very well off in sharing with them one half.

Though Misson's Ship pass'd for a French Man of War, yet his Generosity in letting the Prize go, gave the English Grounds to suspect the Truth, neither the Ship nor Cargoe being of Use to such as were upon the grand Account.

When they had lost all Hopes of the St. Joseph, they coasted along the North-Side of Cuba, and the Victoire growing now foul, they ran into a Landlock'd Bay on the East North-East Point, where they hove her down by Boats and Guns, though they could not pretend to heave her Keel out; however, they scraped and tallowed as far as they could go; they, for this Reason, many of them repented they had let the last Prize go, by which they might have careened.

When they had righted the Ship, and put every Thing on Board, they consulted upon the Course they should steer. Upon this the Council divided. The Captain and Caraccioli were for stretching over to the African, and the others for the New-England Coast, alledging, that the Ship had a foul Bottom, and was not fit for the Voyage; and that if they met with contrary Winds, and bad Weather, their Stock of Provision might fall short; and that as they were not far from the English Settlement of Carolina, they might either on that or the Coast of Virginia, Maryland, Pensylvania, New-York, or New-England, intercept ships which traded to the Islands with Provisions, and by that Means provide themselves with Bread, Flower, and other Necessaries. An Account of the Provisions were taken, and finding they had Provisions for four Months. Captain Misson called all Hands upon Deck, and told them, as the Council differed in the Course they should steer, he thought it reasonable to have it put to the Vote of the whole Company. That for his Part, he was for going to the Coast of Guiney, where they might reasonably expect to meet with valuable Prizes; but should they fail in their Expectation one Way, they would be sure of having it answered another; for they could then throw themselves in that of the East- India Ships, and he need not tell them, that the outward bound dreined Europe of what Money they drew from America. He then gave the Sentiments of those who were against him, and their Reasons, and begg'd that every one would give his Opinion and Vote according as he thought most conducive to the Good of all. That he should be far from taking it ill if they should reject what he had proposed, since he had no private Views to serve. The Majority of Votes fell on the Captain's Side, and they accordingly shaped their Course for the Coast of Guiney, in which Voyage nothing remarkable happened. On their Arrival on the Gold-Coast, they fell in with the Nieuwstadt of Amsterdam, a Ship of 18 Guns, commanded by Capt. Blacs, who made a running Fight of five Glasses: This Ship they kept with them, putting on Board 40 Hands, and bringing all the Prisoners on Board the Victoire, they were Forty three in Number, they left Amsterdam with Fifty six, seven were killed in the Engagement, and they had lost six by Sickness and Accidents, one falling overboard, and one being taken by a Shark going overboard in a Calm.

The Nieuwstadt had some Gold-Dust on Board, to the Value of about 2000 l. Sterling, and a few Slaves to the Number of Seventeen, for she had but begun to Trade; the Slaves were a strengthening of their Hands, for the Captain order'd them to be cloathed out of Dutch Mariners Chests, and told his Men, 'That the Trading for those of our own Species, cou'd never be agreeable to the Eyes of divine Justice: That no Man had Power or the Liberty of another; and while those who profess'd a more enlightened Knowledge of the Deity, sold Men like Beasts; they prov'd that their Religion was no more than Grimace, and that they differ'd from the Barbarians in Name only, since their Practice was in nothing more humane: For his Part, and he hop'd, he spoke the Sentiments of all his brave Companions, he had not exempted his Neck from the galling Yoak of Slavery, and asserted his own Liberty, to enslave others. That however, these Men were distinguish'd from the Europeans by their Colour, Customs, or religious Rites, they were the Work of the same omnipotent Being, and endued with equal Reason: Wherefore, he desired they might be treated like Freemen (for he wou'd banish even the Name of Slavery from among them)' and divided into Messes among them, to the End they might the sooner learn their Language, be sensible of the Obligation they had to them, and more capable and zealous to defend that Liberty they owed to their Justice and Humanity.

This Speech of Misson's was received with general Applause, and the Ship rang with vive le Capitain Misson. Long live Capt. Misson. The Negroes were divided among the French, one to a Mess, who, by their Gesticulations, shew'd they were gratefully sensible of their being delivered from their Chains. Their Ship growing very foul, and going heavily through the Water, they run into the River of Lagoa, where they hove her down, taking out such Planks as had suffer'd most by the Worms, and substituting new in their Room.

After this they careened the Prize, and so put out to Sea, steering to the Southward, and keeping along the Coast, but met with Nothing. All this while, the greatest Decorum and Regularity was observed on Board the Victoire; but the Dutch Prisoners Example began to lead 'em into Swearing and Drunkenness, which the Captain remarking, thought it was best to nip these Vices in the Bud; and calling both the French and Dutch upon Deck, he address'd himself to the former, desiring their Captain, who spoke French excellently well, to interpret what he said to those who did not understand him. He told them, 'before he had the Misfortune of having them on Board, his Ears were never grated with hearing the Name of the great Creator prophaned, tho' he, to his Sorrow, had often since heard his own Men guilty of that Sin, which administer'd neither Profit nor Pleasure, and might draw upon them a severe Punishment: That if they had a just Idea of that great Being, they wou'd never mention him, but they wou'd immediately reflect on his Purity and their own Vileness. That we so easily took Impression from our Company, that the Spanish Proverb says, let a Hermit and a Thief live together, the Thief wou'd become Hermit, or the Hermit Thief: That he saw this verified in his Ship, for he cou'd attribute the Oaths and Curses he had heard among his brave Companions, to nothing but the odious Example of the Dutch: That this was not the only Vice they had introduced, for before they were on Board, his Men were Men, but he found by their beastly Pattern they were degenerated into Brutes, by drowning that only Faculty, which distinguishes between Man and Beast, Reason. That as he had the Honour to command them, he could not see them run into these odious Vices without, a sincere Concern, as he had a paternal Affection for them; and he should reproach himself as neglectful of the common Good, if he did not admonish them; and as by the Post which they had honour'd him, he was obliged to have a watchful Eye over their general Interest; he was obliged to tell them his Sentiments were, that the Dutch allured them to a dissolute Way of Life, that they might take some Advantage over them: Wherefore, as his brave Companions, he was assured, wou'd be guided by Reason, he gave the Dutch Notice, that the first whom he catch'd either with an Oath in his Mouth or Liquor in his Head, should be brought to the Geers, whipped and pickled, for an Example to the rest of his Nation: As to his Friends, his Companions, his Children, those gallant, those generous, noble, and heroick Souls he had the Honour to command, he entreated them to allow a small Time for Reflection, and to consider how little Pleasure sure, and how much Danger, might flow from imitating the Vices of their Enemies; and that they would among themselves, make a Law for the Suppression of what would otherwise estrange them from the Source of Life, and consequently leave them destitute of his Protection.'

It is not to be imagined what Efficacy this Speech had on both Nations: The Dutch grew continent in Fear of Punishment, and the French in Fear of being reproach'd by their good Captain, for they never mentioned him without this Epithet. Upon the Coast of Angola, they met with a second Dutch Ship, the Cargo of which consisted of Silk and Woolen Stuffs, Cloath, Lace, Wine, Brandy, Oyl, Spice, and hard Ware; the Prize gave Chase and engaged her, but upon the coming up of the Victoire she struck. This Ship opportunely came in their Way, and gave full Employ to the Taylors, who were on Board, for the whole Crew began to be out at Elbows: They plundered her of what was of Use to their own Ship, and then sunk her.

The Captain having about ninety Prisoners on Board, proposed the giving them the Prize, with what was necessary for their Voyage, and sending them away; which being agreed to, they shifted her Ammunition on Board the Victoire, and giving them Provision to carry them to the Settlements the Dutch have on the Coast, Misson called them up, told them what was his Design, and ask'd if any of them was willing to share his Fortune: Eleven Dutch came into him, two of which were Sail- makers, one an Armourer, and one a Carpenter, necessary Hands; the rest he let go, not a little surprised at the Regularity, Tranquillity, and Humanity, which they found among these new fashioned Pyrates.

They had now run the Length of Soldinia Bay about ten Leagues to the Northward of Table Bay. As here is good Water, safe Riding, plenty of Fish and fresh Provision, to be got of the Natives for the Merchandize they had on Board, it was resolved to stay here some little Time for Refreshments. When they had the Bay open, they spied a tall Ship, which instantly got under sail, and hove out English Colours. The Victoire made a clear Ship, and hove out her French Ensign, and a smart Engagement began. The English was a new Ship built for 40 Guns, though she had but 32 mounted, and 90 Hands. Misson gave Orders for boarding, and his Number of fresh Men he constantly poured in, after an obstinate Dispute obliged the English to fly the Decks, and leave the French Masters of their Ship, who promised, and gave them, good Quarters, and stripp'd not a Man.

They found on Board the Prize some Bales of English Broad-Cloath, and about 60000 l. in English Crown Pieces, and Spanish Pieces of Eight. The English Captain was killed in the Engagement, and 14 of his Men: The French lost 12, which was no small Mortification, but did not, however provoke them to use their Prisoners harshly. Captain Misson was sorry for the Death of the Commander, whom he buried on the Shoar, and one of his Men being a Stone-Cutter, he raised a Stone over his Grave with these Words, Icy gist un brave Anglois, Here lies a gallant English Man; when he was buried he made a tripple Discharge of 50 small Arms, and fired Minute Guns.

The English, knowing whose Hands they were fallen into, charm'd with Misson's Humanity, 30 of them, in 3 Days Space, desired to take on with him. He accepted 'em, but at the same Time gave 'em to understand, that in taking on with him they were not to expect they should be indulged in a dissolute and immoral Life. He now divided his Company between the two Ships, and made Caraccioli Captain of the Prize, giving him Officers chosen by the publick Suffrage. The 17 Negroes began to understand a little French, and to be useful Hands, and in less than a Month all the English Prisoners came over to him, except their Officers.

He had two Ships well mann'd with resolute Fellows; they now doubled the Cape, and made the South End of Madagascar, and one of the English Men telling Captain Misson, that the European Ships bound for Surat commonly touch'd at the Island of Johanna, he sent for Captain Caracciola on Board, and it was agreed to cruise off that Island. They accordingly sailed on the West-Side of Madagascar and off the Bay de Diego. About half Seas over between that Bay and the Island of Johanna, they came up with an English East-India Man, which made Signals of Distress as soon as she spy'd Misson and his Prize; they found her sinking by an unexpected Leak, and took all her Men on Board, though they could get little out of her before she went down. The English, who were thus miraculously saved from perishing, desired to be set on Shoar at Johanna, where they hop'd to meet with either a Dutch or English Ship in a little Time, and the mean while they were sure of Relief.

They arrived at Johanna, and were kindly received by the Queen-Regent and her Brother, on account of the English on the one Hand, and of their Strength on the other, which the Queen's Brother, who had the Administration of Affairs, was not able to make Head against, and hoped they might assist him against the King of Mohila, who threaten'd him with a Visit.

This is an Island which is contiguous, in a manner, to Johanna, and lies about N. W. and by N. from it. Caraccioli told Misson he might make his Advantage in widening the Breach between these two little Monarchies, and, by offering his Assistance to that of Johanna, in a manner rule both, For these would count him as their Protector, and those come to any Terms to buy his Friendship, by which Means he would hold the Ballance of Power between them. He followed this

Advice, and offered his Friendship and Assistance to the Queen, who very readily embraced it.

I must advise the Reader, that many of this Island speak English, and that the English Men who were of Misson's Crew, and his Interpreters, told them, their Captain, though not an Englishman, was their Friend and Ally, and a Friend and Brother to the Johanna Men, for they esteem the English beyond all other Nations.

They were supplied by the Queen with all Necessaries of Life, and Misson married her Sister, as Caraccioli did the Daughter of her Brother, whose Armory, which consisted before of no more than two rusty Fire-Locks, and three Pistols, he furnish'd with thirty Fuzils, as many Pair of Pistols, and gave him two Barrels of Powder, and four of Ball.

Several of his Men took Wives, and some requited their Share of the Prizes, which was justly given them, they designing to settle in this Island, but the Number of these did not exceed ten, which Loss was repaired by thirty of the Crew (they had saved from perishing) coming in to him.

While they past their Time in all manner of Diversions the Place would afford them, as hunting, feasting, and visiting the Island, the King of Mohila made a Descent, and alarm'd the whole Country. Misson advised the Queen's Brother not to give him any Impediment, but let him get into the Heart of the Island, and he would take Care to intercept their Return; but the Prince answered, should he follow his Advice the Enemy would do him and the Subjects an irreparable Damage, in destroying the Cocoa Walks, and for that Reason he must endeavour to stop his Progress. Upon this Answer he asked the English who were not under his Command, if they were willing to join him in repelling the Enemies of their common Host, and one and all consenting, he gave them Arms, and mixed them with his own Men, and about the same Number of Johannians, under the Command of Caraccioli and the Queen's Brother, and arming out all his Boats, he went himself to the Westward of the Island, where they made their Descent. The Party which went by Land, fell in with, and beat the Mohilians with great Ease, who were in the greatest Consternation, to find their Retreat cut off by Misson's Boats. The Johannians, whom they had often molested, were so enraged, that they gave Quarter to none, and out of 300 who made the Descent, if Misson and Caraccioli had not interposed, not a Soul had escaped; 113 were taken Prisoners by his Men, and carried on Board his Ships. These he sent fate to Mohila, with a Message to the King, to desire he would make Peace with his Friend and Ally the King of Johanna; but that Prince, little affected with the Service done him in the Preservation of his Subjects, sent him Word he took Laws from none, and knew when to make War and Peace without his Advice, which he neither asked nor wanted. Misson, irritated by this rude Answer, resolved to transfer the War into his own Country, and accordingly set sail for Mohila, with about 100 Johanna Men. The Shoar, on Sight of the Ships, was filled with Men to hinder a Descent if intended, but the great Guns soon dispersed this Rabble, and under their Cover he landed the Johannians, and an equal Number of French and English. They were met by about 700 Mohilians, who pretended to stop their Passage, but their Darts and Arrows were of little avail against Misson's Fuzils; the first Discharge made a great Slaughter, and about 20 Shells which were thrown among them, put them to a confus'd Flight.

The Party of Europeans and Johannians then marched to their Metropolis, without Resistance, which they reduced to Ashes, and the Johannians cut down all the Cocoa Walks that they could for the Time, for towards Evening they returned to their Ships, and stood off to Sea.

At their Return to Johanna the Queen made a Festival, and magnified the Bravery and Service of her Guests, Friends, and Allies. This Feast lasted four Days, at the Expiration of which Time the Queen's Brother proposed to Captain Misson the making another Descent, in which he would go in Person, and did not doubt subjecting the Mohilians; but this was not the Design of Misson, who had Thoughts of fixing a Retreat on the North West Side of Madagascar, and look'd upon the Feuds between these two Islands advantageous to his Views, and therefore no way his Interest to suffer the one to overcome the other; for while the Variance was kept up, and their Forces pretty much upon a Level, it was evident their Interest would make both Sides caress him; he therefore answer'd, that they ought to deliberate on the Consequences, for they might be deceived in their Hopes, and find the Conquest less easy than they imagined. That the King of Mohilia would be more upon his Guard, and not only intrench himself, but gall them with frequent Ambuscades, by which they must inevitably lose a Number of Men; and, if they were forced to retire with Loss, raise the Courage of the Mohilians, and make them irreconcilable Enemies to the Johannians, and intirely deprive him of the Advantages with which he might now make a Peace, having twice defeated them: That he could not be always with them, and at his leaving Johanna he might expect the King of Mohilia would endeavour to take a bloody Revenge for the late Damages. The Queen gave intirely into Misson's Sentiments.

While this was in Agitation four Mohilians arrived as Ambassadors to propose a Peace. They finding the Johannians upon high Terms, one of them spoke to this Purpose; O ye Johannians, do not conclude from your late Success, that Fortune will be always favourable; she will not always give you the Protection of the Europeans, and without their Help its possible you might now sue for a Peace, which you seem averse to. Remember the Sun rises, comes to its Meridian Height, and stays not there, but declines in a Moment. Let this admonish you to reflect on the constant Revolution of all sublunary Affairs, and the greater is your Glory, the nearer you are to your Declension. We are taught by every Thing we see, that there is no Stability in the World, but Nature is in continual Movement. The Sea, which o'er flows the Sands has its Bounds set, which it cannot pass, which the Moment it has reached, without abiding, returns back to the Bottom of the Deep. Every Herb, every Shrub and Tree, and even our own Bodies, teach us this Lesson, that nothing is durable, or can be counted upon. Time passes away insensibly, one Sun follows another, and brings its Changes with it. To-Day's Globe of Light sees you strengthened by these Europeans elate with victory, and we, who have been used to conquer you, come to ask a Peace. To Morrow's Sun may see you deprived of your present Succours, and the Johannians petitioning us; as therefore we cannot say what to Morrow may bring forth, it would be unwise on uncertain Hopes to forego a certain Advantage, as surely Peace ought to be esteem'd by every wise Man.

Having said this, the Ambassadors withdrew, and were treated by the Queen's Orders. After the Council had concluded, they were again call'd upon, and the Queen told them, that by the Advice of her good Friends, the Europeans, and those of her Council, she agreed to make a Peace, which she wish'd might banish all Memory of former Injuries That they must own the War was begun by them, and that she was far from being the Agressor; she only defended her self in her own Kingdom, which they had often invaded, though, till within few Days, she had never molested their Coasts. If then they really desired to live amicably with her, they must resolve to send two of the King's Children, and ten of the first Nobility, as Hostages, that they might, when they pleased, return, for that was the only Terms on which she would desist prosecuting the Advantages she now had, with the utmost Vigour.

The Ambassadors returned with this Answer, and, about ten Days after, the two Ships appearing upon their Coasts, they sent off to give Notice, that their King comply'd with the Terms proposed, would send the Hostages, and desired a Cessation of all Hostility, and, at the same Time, invited the Commanders on Shoar. The Johanna Men on Board disswaded their accepting the Invitation; but Misson and Caraccioli, fearing nothing, went, but arm'd their Boat's Crew. They were received by the King with Demonstrations of Friendship, and they dined with him under a Tamerane Tree; but when they parted from him, and were returning to their Boats, they were inclosed by, at least, 100 of the Mohilians, who set upon them with the utmost Fury, and, in the first Flight of Arrows, wounded both the Captains, and killed four of their Boat's Crew of eight, who were with them; they, in return, discharged their Pistols with some Execution, and fell in with their Cutlasses; but all their Bravery would have stood them in little Stead, had not the Report of their Pistols alarm'd and brought the rest of their Friends to their Assistance, who took their Fuzils, and coming up while they were engaged, discharged a Volley on the Back of the Assailants, which laid twelve of them dead on the Spot. The Ships hearing this Fire, sent immediately the Yawls and Long-Boats well mann'd. Though the Islanders were a little damp'd in their Courage by this Fire of the Boats Crew, yet they did not give over the Fight, and one of them desperately threw himself upon Caraccioli, and gave him a deep Wound in his Side, with a long Knife, but he paid for the Rashness of the Attempt with his Life, one of the Crew cleaving his Skull. The Yawls and Long-Boats now arrived, and being guided by the Noise, reinforced their Companions, put the Traytors to Flight, and brought off their dead and wounded. The Europeans lost by this Treachery seven slain outright, and eight wounded, six of which recovered.

The Crew were resolved to revenge the Blood of their Officers and Comrades the next Day, and were accordingly on the Point of Landing, when two Canoes came off with two Men bound, the pretended Authors of this Treason, without the King's Knowledge, who had sent 'em that they might receive the Punishment due to their Villany. The Johanna Men on Board were call'd for Interpreters, who having given this Account, added, that the King only sacrificed these Men, but that they should not believe him, for he certainly had given Orders for assassinating the Europeans; and the better Way was to kill all the Mohilians that came in the Canoes as well as the two Prisoners; go back to Johanna, take more of their Countrymen, and give no Peace to Traytors; but Misson was for no such violent Measures, he was averse to every Thing that bore the Face of Cruelty and thought a bloody Revenge, if Necessity did not enforce it, spoke a groveling and timid Soul; he, therefore, sent those of the Canoes back, and bid them tell their King, if before the Evening he sent the Hostages agreed upon, he should give Credit to his Excuse, but if he did not, he should believe him the Author of the late vile Attempt on his Life.

The Canoes went off but returned not with an Answer, wherefore, he bid the Johanna Men tell the two Prisoners that they should be set on Shore the next Morning, and order'd them to acquaint their King, he was no Executioner to put those to Death whom he had condemn'd, but that he should find, he knew how to revenge himself of his Treason. The Prisoners being unbound, threw themselves at his Feet, and begg'd that he would not send them ashore, for they should be surely put to Death, for the Crime they had committed, was, the dissuading the barbarous Action of which they were accused as Authors.

Next Day the two Ships landed 200 Men, under the Cover of their Canon; but that Precaution of bringing their Ships close to the Shore they found needless; not a soul appearing, they march'd two Leagues up the Country, when they saw a Body of Men appear behind some Shrubs; Caraccioli's Lieutenant, who commanded the right Wing, with fifty Men made up to them, but found he had got among Pit Falls artificially cover'd, several of his Men falling into them, which made him halt, and not pursue those Mohilians who made a feint Retreat to ensnare him, thinking it dangerous to proceed farther; and seeing no Enemy would face them, they retired the same Way they came, and getting into their Boats, went on Board the Ships, resolving to return with a strong Reinforcement, and make Descents at one and the same Time in different Parts of the Island. They ask'd the two Prisoners how the Country lay, and what the Soil was on the North Side the Island; and they answer'd it was morass, and the most dangerous Part to attempt, it being a Place where they shelter on any imminent Danger.

The Ships return'd to Johanna, where the greatest Tenderness and Care was shown for the Recovery and Cure of the two Captains and of their Men; they lay six Weeks before they were able to walk the Decks, for neither of them would quit his Ship. Their Johanna Wives expressed a Concern they did not think them capable of, nay, a Wife of one of the wounded Men who died, stood some Time looking upon the Corpse as motionless as a Statue, then embracing it, without shedding a Tear, desired she might take it ashore to wash and bury it; and at the same Time, by an Interpreter, and with a little Mixture of European Language, she had, begg'd her late Husband's Friends would take their Leave of him the next Day.

Accordingly a Number went ashore, and carried with them the Dividend, which fell to his Share, which the Captain order'd to be given his Widow; when she saw the Money, she smil'd, and ask'd if all, all that was for her? Being answered in the affirmative, and what Good will all that shining Dirt do me, if I could with it purchase the Life of my Husband, and call him back from the Grave, I would accept it with Pleasure, but as it is not sufficient to allure him back to this World, I have no Use for it; do with it what you please. Then she desired they would go with her and perform the last Ceremonies to her Husband's dead Body, after their Country Fashion, least he should be displeased, that she could not stay with them, to be a Witness, because she was in haste to go and be married again. She startled the Europeans who heard this latter Part of her Speech so dissonant from the Beginning; however, they followed her, and she led them into a Plantane Walk, where they found a great many Johanna Men and Women, sitting under the Shade of Plantanes, round the Corpse, which lay (as they all sate) on the Ground, covered with Flowers. She embraced them round, and then the Europeans, one by one, and after these Ceremonies, she poured out a Number of bitter Imprecations against the Mohila Men, whose Treachery had darken'd her Husband's Eyes, and made him insensible of her Caresses, who was her first Love, to whom she had given her Heart, with her Virginity. She then proceeded in his Praises, calling him the Joy of Infants, the Love of Virgins, the Delight of the old, and the Wonder of the young, adding, he was strong and beautiful as the Cedar, brave as the Bull, tender as the Kid, and loving as the Ground Turtle; having finished this Oration, not unlike those of the Romans, which the nearest Relation of the deceas'd used to pronounce from the Rostrum, she laid her down by the Side of her Husband, embracing him, and sitting up again, gave herself a deep Wound under the left Breast with a Bayonet, and fell dead on her Husband's Corpse.

The Europeans were astonished at the Tenderness and Resolution of the Girl, for she was not, by what Her Mien spoke her, past seventeen; and they now admired, as much as they had secretly detested her, for saying she was in haste to be married again, the Meaning of which they did not understand.

After the Husband and Wife were buried, the Crew return'd on Board, and gave an Account of what had pass'd; the Captains Wives (for Misson and his were on Board the Bijoux, the Name they had given their Prize from her Make and Gilding) seem'd not in the least surprized, and Caraccioli's Lady only said, she must be of noble Descent, for none but the Families of the Nobility had the Privilege allowed them of following their Husbands on pain, if they transgressed, of being thrown into the Sea, to be eat by Fish; and they knew, that their Souls could not rest as long as any of the Fish, who fed upon them, lived. Misson asked, if they intended to have done the same Thing had they died? We should not, answer'd his Wife, have disgraced our Families; nor is our Tenderness for our Husbands inferior to hers whom you seem to admire.

After their Recovery, Misson proposes a Cruize, on the Coast of Zangueber, which being agreed to, he and Caraccioli took Leave of the Queen and her Brother, and would have left their Wives on the Island, but they could by no Means be induced to the Separation; it was in vain to urge the Shortness of the Time they were to Cruize; they answer'd it was farther than Mohila they intended to go, and if they were miserable in that short Absence, they could never support a longer; and if they would not allow them to keep them Company the Voyage, they must not expect to see them at their Return, if they intended one.

In a Word they were obliged to yield to them, but told them, if the Wives of their Men should insist as strongly on following their Example, their Tenderness, would be their Ruin, and make them a Prey to their Enemies; they answer'd the Queen should prevent that, by ordering no Woman should go on board, and if any were in the Ships, they should return on Shore: This Order was accordingly made, and they set Sail for the River of Mozembique. In about ten Days Cruize after they had left Johanna, and about 15 Leagues to the Eastward of this River, they fell in with a stout Portuguese Ship of 60 Guns, which engaged them from Break of Day till Two in the Afternoon, when the Captain being killed, and a great Number of Men lost, she struck: This proved a very rich Prize, for she had the Value of 250000 L. Sterling on Board, in Gold-Dust. The two Women never quitted the Decks all the Time of the Engagement, neither gave they the least Mark of Fear, except for their Husbands: This Engagement cost them thirty Men, and Caraccioli lost his right Leg; the Slaughter fell mostly on the English, for of the above Number, twenty were of that Nation: The Portuguese lost double the Number. Caraccioli's Wound made them resolve to make the best of their Way for Johanna where the greatest Care was taken of their wounded, not one of whom died, tho' their Number amounted to Twenty seven.

Caraccioli kept his Bed two Months, but Misson seeing him in a fair way of Recovery, took what Hands could be spar'd from the Bijoux, leaving her sufficient for Defence, and went out, having mounted ten of the Portuguese Guns, for he had hitherto carried but thirty, though he had Ports for forty. He stretched over to Madagascar, and coasted along this Island to the Northward, as far as the most northerly Point, when turning back, he enter'd a Bay to the northward of Diego Suares. He run ten Leagues up this Bay, and on the larboard Side found it afforded a large, and safe, Harbour, with plenty of fresh Water. He came here to an Anchor, went ashore and examined into the Nature of the Soil, which he found rich, the Air wholesome, and the Country level. He told his Men, that this was an excellent Place for an Asylum, and that he determined here to fortify and raise a small Town, and make Docks for Shipping, that they might have some Place to call their own; and a Receptacle, when Age or Wounds had render'd them incapable of Hardship, where they might enjoy the Fruits of their Labour, and go to their Graves in Peace. That he would not, however, set about this, till he had the Approbation of the whole Company; and were he sure they would all approve this Design, which he hoped, it being evidently for the general Good, he should not think it adviseable to begin any Works, lest the Natives should, in his Absence, destroy them; but however, as they had nothing upon their Hands, if they were of his Opinion, they might begin to fall and square Timber, ready for the raising a wooden Fort, when they return'd with their Companions.

The Captain's Motion was universally applauded, and in ten Days they fell'd and rough hew'd a hundred and fifty large Trees, without any Interruption from, or seeing any of, the Inhabitants. They fell'd their Timber at the Waters Edge, so that they had not the Trouble of hawling them any way, which would have employ'd a great deal more Time: They returned again, and acquainted their Companions with what they had seen and done, and with the Captain's Resolution, which they one and all came into.

Captain Misson then told the Queen, as he had been serviceable to her in her War with the Island of Mohila, and might continue to be of farther Use, he did not question her lending him Assistance in the settling himself on the Coast of Madagascar, and to that end, furnish him with 300 Men, to help in his Buildings; the Queen answered, she could do nothing without Consent of Council, and that she would assemble her Nobility, and did not question their agreeing to any Thing he could reasonably define, for they were sensible of the Obligations the Johanians had to him. The Council was accordingly called, and Misson's Demand being told, one of the eldest said, he did not think it expedient to comply with it, nor safe to refuse; that they should in agreeing to give him that Assistance, help to raise a Power, which might prove formidable to themselves, by the being so near a Neighbour; and these Men who had lately protected, might, when they found it for their Interest, enslave them. On the other hand, if they did not comply, they had the Power to do them great Damage. That they were to make choice of the least of two possible Evils, for he could prognosticate no Good to Johanna, by their settling near it. Another answered, that many of them had Johanna Wives, that it was not likely they would make Enemies of the Johanna Men at first settling, because their Friendship might be of Use to them; and from their Children there was nothing to be apprehended in the next Generation, for they would be half their own Blood; that in the mean while, if they comply'd with the Request, they might be sure of an Ally, and Protector, against the King of Mohila; wherefore, he was for agreeing to the Demand.

After a long Debate, in which every Inconvenience, and Advantage, was maturely considered, it was agreed to send with him the Number of Men he required, on Condition he should send them back in four Moons, make an Alliance with them, and War against Mohila; this being agreed to, they staid till Caraccioli was thoroughly recovered, then putting the Johannians on board the Portuguese Ship with 40 French and English and 15 Portuguese to work her, and setting Sail, they arrived at the Place where Misson designed his Settlement, which he called Libertalia, and gave the Name of Liberi to his People, desiring in that might be drown'd the distingush'd Names of French, English, Dutch, Africans, &c.

The first Thing they sat about was, the raising a Fort on each Side the Harbour, which they made of an octogon Figure, and having finished and mounted them with 40 Guns taken out of the Portuguese, they raised a Battery on an Angle of ten Guns, and began to raise Houses and Magazines under the Protection of their Forts and Ships; the Portuguese was unrigg'd, and all her Sails and Cordage carefully laid up. While they were very busily employed in the raising a Town, a Party which had often hunted and rambled four or five Leagues off their Settlement, resolved to venture farther into the Country. They made themselves some Huts, at about 4 Leagues distance from their Companions, and travell'd East South East, about 5 Leagues farther into the Country, when they came up with a Black, who was arm'd with a Bow, Arrows, and a Javelin; they with a friendly Appearance engaged the Fellow to lay by his Fear and go with them. They carried him to their Companions, and there entertained him three Days with a great Deal of Humanity, and then returned with him near the Place they found him, made him a Present of a Piece of scarlet Baze, and an Ax; he appeared overjoy'd at the Present, and left them with seeming Satisfaction.

The Hunters imagined that there might be some Village not far off, and observing that he look'd at the Sun, and then took his Way direct South, they travell'd on the same Point of the Compass, and from the Top of a Hill they spied a pretty large Village, and went down to it; the Men came out with their Arms, such as before described, Bows, Arrows, and Javelins, but upon two only of the Whites advancing, with Presents of Axes, and Baze in their Hands, they sent only four to meet them. The Misfortune was, that they could not understand one another, but by their pointing to the Sun, and holding up one Finger, and making one of them go forward, and return again with showing their Circumcision, and pointing up to Heaven with one Finger, they apprehended, they gave them to understand, there was but one God, who had sent one Prophet, and concluded from thence, and their Circumcision they were Mahometans; the Presents were carried to their Chief, and he seem'd to receive them kindly, and by Signs invited the Whites into their Village; but they, remembring the late Treachery of the Mohilians, made Signs for Victuals to be brought them where they were.

More of the History of these Adventurers in another Place.

Dickory Cronke: The Dumb Philosopher, or, Great Britain's Wonder

I. A faithful and very surprising Account how Dickory Cronke, a Tinner's son, in the County of Cornwall, was born Dumb, and continued so for Fifty- eight years; and how, some days before he died, he came to his Speech; with Memoirs of his Life, and the Manner of his Death.

II. A Declaration of his Faith and Principles in Religion; with a Collection of Select Meditations, composed in his Retirement.

III. His Prophetical Observations upon the Affairs of Europe, more particularly of Great Britain, from 1720 to 1729. The whole extracted from his Original Papers, and confirmed by unquestionable Authority.

TO WHICH IS ANNEXED HIS ELEGY, WRITTEN BY A YOUNG CORNISH GENTLEMAN, OF EXETER COLLEGE IN OXFORD.

WITH AN EPITAPH BY ANOTHER HAND.

"Non quis, sed quid."

PREFACE

The formality of a preface to this little book might have been very well omitted, if it were not to gratify the curiosity of some inquisitive people, who, I foresee, will be apt to make objections against the reality of the narrative.

Indeed the public has too often been imposed upon by fictitious stories, and some of a very late date, so that I think myself obliged by the usual respect which is paid to candid and impartial readers, to acquaint them, by way of introduction, with what they are to expect, and what they may depend upon, and yet with this caution too, that it is an indication of ill nature or ill manners, if not both, to pry into a secret that is industriously concealed.

However, that there may be nothing wanting on my part, I do hereby assure the reader, that the papers from whence the following sheets were extracted, are now in town, in the custody of a person of unquestionable reputation, who, I will be bold to say, will not only be ready, but proud, to produce them upon a good occasion, and that I think is as much satisfaction as the nature of this case requires.

As to the performance, it can signify little now to make an apology upon that account, any farther than this, that if the reader pleases he may take notice that what he has now before him was collected from a large bundle of papers, most of which were writ in shorthand, and very ill-digested. However, this may be relied upon, that though the language is something altered, and now and then a word thrown in to help the expression, yet strict care has been taken to speak the author's mind, and keep as close as possible to the meaning of the original. For the design, I think there is nothing need be said in vindication of that. Here is a dumb philosopher introduced to a wicked and degenerate generation, as a proper emblem of virtue and morality; and if the world could be persuaded to look upon him with candour and impartiality, and then to copy after him, the editor has gained his end, and would think himself sufficiently recompensed for his present trouble.

PART I

Among the many strange and surprising events that help to fill the accounts of this last century, I know none that merit more an entire credit, or are more fit to be preserved and handed to posterity than those I am now going to lay before the public.

Dickory Cronke, the subject of the following narrative, was born at a little hamlet, near St. Columb, in Cornwall, on the 29th of May, 1660, being the day and year in which King Charles the Second was restored. His parents were of mean extraction, but honest, industrious people, and well beloved in their neighbourhood. His father's chief business was to work at the tin mines; his mother stayed at home to look after the children, of which they had several living at the same time. Our Dickory was the youngest, and being but a sickly child, had always a double portion of her care and tenderness.

It was upwards of three years before it was discovered that he was born dumb, the knowledge of which at first gave his mother great uneasiness, but finding soon after that he had his hearing, and all his other senses to the greatest perfection, her grief began to abate, and she resolved to have him brought up as well as their circumstances and his capacity would permit.

As he grew, notwithstanding his want of speech, he every day gave some instance of a ready genius, and a genius much superior to the country children, insomuch that several gentlemen in the neighbourhood took particular notice of him, and would often call him Restoration Dick, and give him money.

When he came to be eight years of age, his mother agreed with a person in the next village, to teach him to read and write, both which, in a very short time, he acquired to such perfection, especially the latter, that he not only taught his own brothers and sisters, but likewise several young men and women in the neighbourhood, which often brought him in small sums, which he always laid out in such necessaries as he stood most in need of.

In this state he continued till he was about twenty, and then he began to reflect how scandalous it was for a young man of his age and circumstances to live idle at home, and so resolves to go with his father to the mines, to try if he could get something towards the support of himself and the family; but being of a tender constitution, and often sick, he soon perceived that sort of business was too hard for him, so was forced to return home and continue in his former station; upon which he grew exceeding melancholy, which his mother observing, she comforted him in the best manner she could, telling him that if it should please God to take her away, she had something left in store for him, which would preserve him against public want.

This kind assurance from a mother whom he so dearly loved gave him some, though not an entire satisfaction; however, he resolves to acquiesce under it till Providence should order something for him more to his content and advantage, which, in a short time happened according to his wish. The manner was thus:-

One Mr. Owen Parry, a Welsh gentleman of good repute, coming from Bristol to Padstow, a little seaport in the county of Cornwall, near the place where Dickory dwelt, and hearing much of this dumb man's perfections, would needs have him sent for; and finding, by his significant gestures and all outward appearances that he much exceeded the character that the country gave of him, took a mighty liking to him, insomuch that he told him, if he would go with him into Pembrokeshire, he would be kind to him, and take care of him as long as he lived.

This kind and unexpected offer was so welcome to poor Dickory, that without any farther consideration, he got a pen and ink and writ a note, and in a very handsome and submissive manner returned him thanks for his favour, assuring him he would do his best to continue and improve it; and that he would be ready to wait upon him whenever he should be pleased to command.

To shorten the account as much as possible, all things were concluded to their mutual satisfaction, and in about a fortnight's time they set forward for Wales, where Dickory, notwithstanding his dumbness, behaved himself with so much diligence and affability, that he not only gained the love of the family where he lived, but of everybody round him.

In this station he continued till the death of his master, which happened about twenty years afterwards; in all which time, as has been confirmed by several of the family, he was never observed to be any ways disguised by drinking, or to be guilty of any of the follies and irregularities incident to servants in gentlemen's houses. On the contrary, when he had any spare time, his constant custom was to retire with some good book into a private place within call, and there employ himself in reading, and then writing down his observations upon what he read.

After the death of his master, whose loss afflicted him to the last degree, one Mrs. Mary Mordant, a gentlewoman of great virtue and piety, and a very good fortune, took him into her service, and carried him with her, first to Bath, and then to Bristol, where, after a lingering distemper, which continued for about four years, she died likewise.

Upon the loss of his mistress, Dickory grew again exceeding melancholy and disconsolate; at length, reflecting that death is but a common debt which all mortals owe to nature, and must be paid sooner or later, he became a little better satisfied, and so determines to get together what he had saved in his service, and then to return to his native country, and there finish his life in privacy and retirement.

Having been, as has been mentioned, about twenty-four years a servant, and having, in the interim, received two legacies, viz., one of thirty pounds, left him by his master, and another of fifteen pounds by his mistress, and being always very frugal, he had got by him in the whole upwards of sixty pounds. This, thinks he, with prudent management, will be enough to support me as long as I live, and so I'll e'en lay aside all thoughts of future business, and make the best of my way to Cornwall, and there find out some safe and solitary retreat, where I may have liberty to meditate and make my melancholy observations upon the several occurrences of human life.

This resolution prevailed so far, that no time was let slip to get everything in readiness to go with the first ship. As to his money, he always kept that locked up by him, unless he sometimes lent it to a friend without interest, for he had a mortal hatred to all sorts of usury or extortion. His books, of which he had a considerable quantity, and some of them very good ones, together with his other equipage, he got packed up, that nothing might be wanting against the first opportunity.

In a few days he heard of a vessel bound to Padstow, the very port he wished to go to, being within four or five miles of the place where he was born. When he came thither, which was in less than a week, his first business was to inquire after the state of his family. It was some time before he could get any information of them, until an old man that knew his father and mother, and remembered they had a son was born dumb, recollected him, and after a great deal of difficulty, made him understand that all his family except his youngest sister were dead, and that she was a widow, and lived at a little town called St. Helen's, about ten miles farther in the country.

This doleful news, we must imagine, must be extremely shocking, and add a new sting to his former affliction; and here it was that he began to exercise the philosopher, and to demonstrate himself both a wise and a good man. All these things, thinks he, are the will of Providence, and must not be disputed; and so he bore up under them with an entire resignation, resolving that, as soon as he could find a place where he might deposit his trunk and boxes with safety, he would go to St. Helen's in quest of his sister.

How his sister and he met, and how transported they were to see each other after so long an interval, I think is not very material. It is enough for the present purpose that Dickory soon recollected his sister, and she him; and after a great many endearing tokens of love and tenderness, he wrote to her, telling her that he believed Providence had bestowed on him as much as would support him as long as he lived, and that if she thought proper he would come and spend the remainder of his days with her.

The good woman no sooner read his proposal than she accepted it, adding, withal, that she could wish her entertainment was better; but if he would accept of it as it was, she would do her best to make everything easy, and that he should be welcome upon his own terms, to stay with her as long as he pleased.

This affair being so happily settled to his full satisfaction, he returns to Padstow to fetch the things he had left behind him, and the next day came back to St. Helen's, where, according to his own proposal, he continued to the day of his death, which happened upon the 29th of May, 1718, about the same hour in which he was born.

Having thus given a short detail of the several periods of his life, extracted chiefly from the papers which he left behind him, I come in the next place to make a few observations how he managed himself and spent his time toward the latter part of it.

His constant practice, both winter and summer, was to rise and set with the sun; and if the weather would permit, he never failed to walk in some unfrequented place, for three hours, both morning and evening, and there it is supposed he composed the following meditations. The chief part of his sustenance was milk, with a little bread boiled in it, of which in the morning, after his walk, he would eat the quantity of a pint, and sometimes more. Dinners he never eat any; and at night he would only have a pretty large piece of bread, and drink a draught of good spring water; and after this method he lived during the whole time he was at St. Helen's. It is observed of him that he never slept out of a bed, nor never lay awake in one; which I take to be an argument, not only of a strong and healthful constitution, but of a mind composed and calm, and entirely free from the ordinary disturbances of human life. He never gave the least signs of complaint or dissatisfaction at anything, unless it was when he heard the tinners swear, or saw them drunk; and then, too, he would get out of the way as soon as he had let them see, by some significant signs, how scandalous and ridiculous they made themselves; and against the next time he met them, would be sure to have a paper ready written, wherein he would represent the folly of drunkenness, and the dangerous consequences that generally attended it.

Idleness was his utter aversion, and if at any time he had finished the business of the day, and was grown weary of reading and writing, in which he daily spent six hours at least, he would certainly find something either within doors or without, to employ himself.

Much might be said both with regard to the wise and regular management, and the prudent methods he took to spend his time well towards the declension of his life; but, as his history may perhaps be shortly published at large by a better hand, I shall only observe in the general, that he was a person of great wisdom and sagacity. He understood nature beyond the ordinary capacity, and, if he had had a competency of learning suitable to his genius, neither this nor the former ages would have produced a better philosopher or a greater man.

I come next to speak of the manner of his death and the consequences thereof, which are, indeed, very surprising, and, perhaps, not altogether unworthy a general observation. I shall relate them as briefly as I can, and leave every one to believe or disbelieve as he thinks proper.

Upon the 26th of May, 1718, according to his usual method, about four in the afternoon, he went out to take his evening walk; but before he could reach the place he intended, he was siezed with an apoplectic fit, which only gave him liberty to sit down under a tree, where, in an instant, he was deprived of all manner of sense and motion, and so he continued, as appears by his own confession afterwards, for more than fourteen hours.

His sister, who knew how exact he was in all his methods, finding him stay a considerable time beyond the usual hour, concludes that some misfortune must needs have happened to him, or he would certainly have been at home before. In short, she went immediately to all the places he was wont to frequent, but nothing could be heard or seen of him till the next morning, when a young man, as he was going to work, discovered him, and went home and told his sister that her brother lay in such a place, under a tree, and, as he believed had been robbed and murdered.

The poor woman, who had all night been under the most dreadful apprehensions, was now frightened and confounded to the last degree. However, recollecting herself, and finding there was no remedy, she got two or three of her neighbours to bear her company, and so hastened with the young man to the tree, where she found her brother lying in the same posture that he had described.

The dismal object at first view startled and surprised everybody present, and filled them full of different notions and conjectures. But some of the company going nearer to him, and finding that he had lost nothing, and that there were no marks of any violence to be discovered about him, they conclude that it must be an apoplectic or some other sudden fit that had surprised him in his walk, upon which his sister and the rest began to feel his hands and face, and observing that he was still warm, and that there were some symptoms of life yet remaining, they conclude that the best way was to carry him home to bed, which was accordingly done with the utmost expedition.

When they had got him into the bed, nothing was omitted that they could think of to bring him to himself, but still he continued utterly insensible for about six hours. At the sixth hour's end he began to move a little, and in a very short time was so far recovered, to the great astonishment of everybody about him, that he was able to look up, and to make a sign to his sister to bring him a cup of water.

After he had drunk the water he soon perceived that all his faculties were returned to their former stations, and though his strength was very much abated by the length and rigour of the fit, yet his intellects were as strong and vigorous as ever.

His sister observing him to look earnestly upon the company, as if he had something extraordinary to communicate to them, fetched him a pen and ink and a sheet of paper, which, after a short pause, he took, and wrote as follows:-

"Dear sister,

"I have now no need of pen, ink, and paper, to tell you my meaning. I find the strings that bound up my tongue, and hindered me from speaking, are unloosed, and I have words to express myself as freely and distinctly as any other person. From whence this strange and unexpected event should proceed, I must not

pretend to say, any farther than this, that it is doubtless the hand of Providence that has done it, and in that I ought to acquiesce. Pray let me be alone for two or three hours, that I may be at liberty to compose myself, and put my thoughts in the best order I can before I leave them behind me."

The poor woman, though extremely startled at what her brother had written, yet took care to conceal it from the neighbours, who, she knew, as well as she, must be mightily surprised at a thing so utterly unexpected. Says she, my brother desires to be alone; I believe he may have something in his mind that disturbs him. Upon which the neighbours took their leave and returned home, and his sister shut the door, and left him alone to his private contemplations.

After the company were withdrawn he fell into a sound sleep, which lasted from two till six, and his sister, being apprehensive of the return of his fit, came to the bedside, and, asking softly if he wanted anything, he turned about to her and spoke to this effect: Dear sister, you see me not only recovered out of a terrible fit, but likewise that I have the liberty of speech, a blessing that I have been deprived of almost sixty years, and I am satisfied you are sincerely joyful to find me in the state I now am in; but, alas! it is but a mistaken kindness. These are things but of short duration, and if they were to continue for a hundred years longer, I can't see how I should be anyways the better.

I know the world too well to be fond of it, and am fully satisfied that the difference between a long and a short life is insignificant, especially when I consider the accidents and company I am to encounter. Do but look seriously and impartially upon the astonishing notion of time and eternity, what an immense deal has run out already, and how infinite it is still in the future; do but seriously and deliberately consider this, and you will find, upon the whole, that three days and three ages of life come much to the same measure and reckoning.

As soon as he had ended his discourse upon the vanity and uncertainty of human life, he looked steadfastly upon her. Sister, says he, I conjure you not to be disturbed at what I am going to tell you, which you will undoubtedly find to be true in every particular. I perceive my glass is run, and I have now no more to do in this world but to take my leave of it; for to-morrow about this time my speech will be again taken from me, and, in a short time, my fit will return; and the next day, which I understand is the day on which I came into this troublesome world, I shall exchange it for another, where, for the future, I shall for ever be free from all manner of sin and sufferings.

The good woman would have made him a reply, but he prevented her by telling her he had no time to hearken to unnecessary complaints or animadversions. I have a great many things in my mind, says he, that require a speedy and serious consideration. The time I have to stay is but short, and I have a great deal of important business to do in it. Time and death are both in my view, and seem both to call aloud to me to make no delay. I beg of you, therefore, not to disquiet yourself or me. What must be, must be. The decrees of Providence are eternal and unalterable; why, then, should we torment ourselves about that which we cannot remedy?

I must confess, my dear sister, I owe you many obligations for your exemplary fondness to me, and do solemnly assure you I shall retain the sense of them to the last moment. All that I have to request of you is, that I may be alone for this night. I have it in my thoughts to leave some short observations behind me, and likewise to discover some things of great weight which have been revealed to me, which may perhaps be of some use hereafter to you and your friends. What credit they may meet with I cannot say, but depend the consequence, according to their respective periods, will account for them, and vindicate them against the supposition of falsity and mere suggestion.

Upon this, his sister left him till about four in the morning, when coming to his bedside to know if he wanted anything, and how he had rested, he made her this answer; I have been taking a cursory view of my life, and though I find myself exceedingly deficient in several particulars, yet I bless God I cannot find I have any just grounds to suspect my pardon. In short, says he, I have spent this night with more inward pleasure and true satisfaction than ever I spent a night through the whole course of my life.

After he had concluded what he had to say upon the satisfaction that attended an innocent and well-spent life, and observed what a mighty consolation it was to persons, not only under the apprehension, but even in the very agonies of death itself, he desired her to bring him his usual cup of water, and then to help him on with his clothes, that he might sit up, and so be in a better posture to take his leave of her and her friends.

When she had taken him up, and placed him at a table where he usually sat, he desired her to bring him his box of papers, and after he had collected those he intended should be preserved, he ordered her to bring a candle, that he might see the rest burnt. The good woman seemed at first to oppose the burning of his papers, till he told her they were only useless trifles, some unfinished observations which he had made in his youthful days, and were not fit to be seen by her, or anybody that should come after him.

After he had seen his papers burnt, and placed the rest in their proper order, and had likewise settled all his other affairs, which was only fit to be done between himself and his sister, he desired her to call two or three of the most reputable neighbours, not only to be witnesses of his will, but likewise to hear what he had farther to communicate before the return of his fit, which he expected very speedily.

His sister, who had beforehand acquainted two or three of her confidants with all that had happened, was very much rejoiced to hear her brother make so unexpected a concession; and accordingly, without any delay or hesitation, went directly into the neighbourhood, and brought home her two select friends, upon whose secrecy and sincerity she knew she might depend upon all accounts.

In her absence he felt several symptoms of the approach of his fit, which made him a little uneasy, lest it should entirely seize him before he had perfected his will, but that apprehension was quickly removed by her speedy return. After she had introduced her friends into his chamber, he proceeded to express himself in the following manner; Dear sister, you now see your brother upon the brink of eternity; and as the words of dying persons are commonly the most regarded, and make deepest impressions, I cannot suspect but you will suffer the few I am about to say to have always some place in your thoughts, that they may be ready for you to make use of upon any occasion.

Do not be fond of anything on this side of eternity, or suffer your interest to incline you to break your word, quit your modesty, or to do anything that will not bear the light, and look the world in the face. For be assured of this; the person that values the virtue of his mind and the dignity of his reason, is always easy and well fortified both against death and misfortune, and is perfectly indifferent about the length or shortness of his life. Such a one is solicitous about nothing but his own conduct, and for fear he should be deficient in the duties of religion, and the respective functions of reason and prudence.

Always go the nearest way to work. Now, the nearest way through all the business of human life, are the paths of religion and honesty, and keeping those as directly as you can, you avoid all the dangerous precipices that often lie in the road, and sometimes block up the passage entirely.

Remember that life was but lent at first, and that the remainder is more than you have reason to expect, and consequently ought to be managed with more than ordinary diligence. A wise man spends every day as if it were his last; his hourglass is always in his hand, and he is never guilty of sluggishness or insincerity.

He was about to proceed, when a sudden symptom of the return of his fit put him in mind that it was time to get his will witnessed, which was no sooner done but he took it up and gave it to his sister, telling her that though all he had was hers of right, yet he thought it proper, to prevent even a possibility of a dispute, to write down his mind in the nature of a will, wherein I have given you, says he, the little that I have left, except my books and papers, which, as soon as I am dead, I desire may be delivered to Mr. Anthony Barlow, a near relation of my worthy master, Mr. Owen Parry.

This Mr. Anthony Barlow was an old contemplative Welsh gentleman, who, being under some difficulties in his own country, was forced to come into Cornwall and take sanctuary among the tinners. Dickory, though he kept himself as retired as possible, happened to meet him one day upon his walks, and presently remembered that he was the very person that used frequently to come to visit his master while he lived in Pembrokeshire, and so went to him, and by signs made him understand who he was.

The old gentleman, though at first surprised at this unexpected interview, soon recollected that he had formerly seen at Mr. Parry's a dumb man, whom they used to call the dumb philosopher, so concludes immediately that consequently this must be he. In short, they soon made themselves known to each other; and from that time contracted a strict friendship and a correspondence by letters, which for the future they mutually managed with the greatest exactness and familiarity.

But to leave this as a matter not much material, and to return to our narrative. By this time Dickory's speech began to falter, which his sister observing, put him in mind that he would do well to make some declaration of his faith and principles of religion, because some reflections had been made upon him upon the account of his neglect, or rather his refusal, to appear at any place of public worship.

"Dear sister," says he, "you observe very well, and I wish the continuance of my speech for a few moments, that I might make an ample declaration upon that account. But I find that cannot be; my speech is leaving me so fast that I can only tell you that I have always lived, and now die, an unworthy member of the ancient catholic and apostolic church; and as to my faith and principles, I refer you to my papers, which, I hope, will in some measure vindicate me against the reflections you mention."

He had hardly finished his discourse to his sister and her two friends, and given some short directions relating to his burial, but his speech left him; and what makes the thing the more remarkable, it went away, in all appearance, without giving him any sort of pain or uneasiness.

When he perceived that his speech was entirely vanished, and that he was again in his original state of dumbness, he took his pen as formerly and wrote to his sister, signifying that whereas the sudden loss of his speech had deprived him of the opportunity to speak to her and her friends what he intended, he would leave it for them in writing, and so desired he might not be disturbed till the return of his fit, which he expected in six hours at farthest. According to his desire they all left him, and then, with the greatest resignation imaginable, he wrote down the meditations following:

PART II

An Abstract of his Faith, and the Principles of his Religion, which begins thus:

Dear Sister; I thank you for putting me in mind to make a declaration of my faith, and the principles of my religion. I find, as you very well observe, I have been under some reflections upon that account, and therefore I think it highly requisite that I set that matter right in the first place. To begin, therefore, with my faith, in which I intend to be as short and as comprehensive as I can:

1. I most firmly believe that it was the eternal will of God, and the result of his infinite wisdom, to create a world, and for the glory of his majesty to make several sorts of creatures in order and degree one after another; that is to say, angels, or pure immortal spirits; men, consisting of immortal spirits and matter, having rational and sensitive souls; brutes, having mortal and sensitive souls; and mere vegetatives, such as trees, plants, &c.; and these creatures so made do, as it were, clasp the higher and lower world together.

2. I believe the holy Scriptures, and everything therein contained, to be the pure and essential word of God; and that, according to these sacred writings, man, the lord and prince of the creation, by his disobedience in Paradise, forfeited his

innocence and the dignity of his nature, and subjected himself and all his posterity to sin and misery.

3. I believe and am fully and entirely satisfied, that God the Father, out of his infinite goodness and compassion to mankind, was pleased to send his only Son, the second person in the holy and undivided Trinity, to meditate for him, and to procure his redemption and eternal salvation.

4. I believe that God the Son, out of his infinite love, and for the glory of the Deity, was pleased voluntarily and freely to descend from heaven, and to take our nature upon him, and to lead an exemplary life of purity, holiness, and perfect obedience, and at last to suffer an ignominious death upon the cross, for the sins of the whole world, and to rise again the third day for our justification.

5. I believe that the Holy Ghost out of his infinite goodness was pleased to undertake the office of sanctifying us with his divine grace, and thereby assisting us with faith to believe, will to desire, and power to do all those things that are required of us in this world, in order to entitle us to the blessings of just men made perfect in the world to come.

6. I believe that these three persons are of equal power, majesty, and duration, and that the Godhead of the Father, of the Son, and of the Holy Ghost is all one, and that they are equally uncreate, incomprehensible, eternal, and almighty; and that none is greater or less than the other, but that every one hath one and the same divine nature and perfections.

These, sister, are the doctrines which have been received and practised by the best men of every age, from the beginning of the Christian religion to this day, and it is upon this I ground my faith and hopes of salvation, not doubting but, if my life and practice have been answerable to them, that I shall be quickly translated out of this kingdom of darkness, out of this world of sorrow, vexation and confusion, into that blessed kingdom, where I shall cease to grieve and to suffer, and shall be happy to all eternity.

As to my principles in religion, to be as brief as I can, I declare myself to be a member of Christ's church, which I take to be a universal society of all Christian people, distributed under lawful governors and pastors into particular churches, holding communion with each other in all the essentials of the Christian faith, worship, and discipline; and among these I look upon the Church of England to be the chief and best constituted.

The Church of England is doubtless the great bulwark of the ancient Catholic or Apostolic faith all over the world; a church that has all the spiritual advantages that the nature of a church is capable of. From the doctrine and principles of the Church of England, we are taught loyalty to our prince, fidelity to our country, and justice to all mankind; and therefore, as I look upon this to be one of the most excellent branches of the Church Universal, and stands, as it were, between superstition and hypocrisy, I therefore declare, for the satisfaction of you and your friends, as I have always lived so I now die, a true and sincere, though a most unworthy member of it. And as to my discontinuance of my attendance at the public worship, I refer you to my papers, which I have left with my worthy friend, Mr. Barlow. And thus, my dear sister, I have given you a short account of my faith, and the principles of my religion. I come, in the next place, to lay before you a few meditations and observations I have at several times collected together, more particularly those since my retirement to St. Helen's.

Meditations and Observations relating to the Conduct of Human Life in general.

1. Remember how often you have neglected the great duties of religion and virtue, and slighted the opportunities that Providence has put into your hands; and, withal, that you have a set period assigned you for the management of the affairs of human life; and then reflect seriously that, unless you resolve immediately to improve the little remains, the whole must necessarily slip away insensibly, and then you are lost beyond recovery.

2. Let an unaffected gravity, freedom, justice, and sincerity shine through all your actions, and let no fancies and chimeras give the least check to those excellent qualities. This is an easy task, if you will but suppose everything you do to be your last, and if you can keep your passions and appetites from crossing your reason. Stand clear of rashness, and have nothing of insincerity or self-love to infect you.

3. Manage all your thoughts and actions with such prudence and circumspection as if you were sensible you were just going to step into the grave. A little thinking will show a man the vanity and uncertainty of all sublunary things, and enable him to examine maturely the manner of dying; which, if duly abstracted from the terror of the idea, will appear nothing more than an unavoidable appendix of life itself, and a pure natural action.

4. Consider that ill-usage from some sort of people is in a manner necessary, and therefore do not be disquieted about it, but rather conclude that you and your enemy are both marching off the stage together, and that in a little time your very memories will be extinguished.

5. Among your principal observations upon human life, let it be always one to take notice what a great deal both of time and ease that man gains who is not troubled with the spirit of curiosity, who lets his neighbours' affairs alone, and confines his inspections to himself, and only takes care of honesty and a good conscience.

6. If you would live at your ease, and as much as possible be free from the incumbrances of life, manage but a few things at once, and let those, too, be such as are absolutely necessary. By this rule you will draw the bulk of your business into a narrow compass, and have the double pleasure of making your actions good, and few into the bargain.

7. He that torments himself because things do not happen just as he would have them, is but a sort of ulcer in the world; and he that is selfish, narrow-souled, and sets up for a separate interest, is a kind of voluntary outlaw, and disincorporates himself from mankind.

8. Never think anything below you which reason and your own circumstances require, and never suffer yourself to be deterred by the ill-grounded notions of censure and reproach; but when honesty and conscience prompt you to say or do anything, do it boldly; never balk your resolution or start at the consequence.

9. If a man does me an injury, what is that to me? It is his own action, and let him account for it. As for me, I am in my proper station, and only doing the business that Providence has allotted; and withal, I ought to consider that the best way to revenge, is not to imitate the injury.

10. When you happen to be ruffled and put out of humour by any cross accident, retire immediately into your reason, and do not suffer your passion to overrule you a moment; for the sooner you recover yourself now, the better you will be able to guard yourself for the future.

11. Do not be like those ill-natured people that, though they do not love to give a good word to their contemporaries, yet are mighty fond of their own commendations. This argues a perverse and unjust temper, and often exposes the authors to scorn and contempt.

12. If any one convinces you of an error, change your opinion and thank him for it: truth and information are your business, and can never hurt anybody. On the contrary, he that is proud and stubborn, and wilfully continues in a mistake, it is he that receives the mischief.

13. Because you see a thing difficult, do not instantly conclude it to be impossible to master it. Diligence and industry are seldom defeated. Look, therefore, narrowly into the thing itself, and what you observe proper and practicable in another, conclude likewise within your own power.

14. The principal business of human life is run through within the short compass of twenty-four hours; and when you have taken a deliberate view of the present age, you have seen as much as if you had begun with the world, the rest being nothing else but an endless round of the same thing over and over again.

15. Bring your will to your fate, and suit your mind to your circumstances. Love your friends and forgive your enemies, and do justice to all mankind, and you will be secure to make your passage easy, and enjoy most of the comforts human life is capable to afford you.

16. When you have a mind to entertain yourself in your retirements, let it be with the good qualifications of your friends and acquaintance. Think with pleasure and satisfaction upon the honour and bravery of one, the modesty of another, the generosity of a third, and so on; there being nothing more pleasant and diverting than the lively images and the advantages of those we love and converse with.

17. As nothing can deprive you of the privileges of your nature, or compel you to act counter to your reason, so nothing can happen to you but what comes from Providence, and consists with the interest of the universe.

18. Let people's tongues and actions be what they will, your business is to have honour and honesty in your view. Let them rail, revile, censure, and condemn, or make you the subject of their scorn and ridicule, what does it all signify? You have one certain remedy against all their malice and folly, and that is, to live so that nobody shall believe them.

19. Alas, poor mortals! did we rightly consider our own state and condition, we should find it would not be long before we have forgot all the world, and to be even, that all the world will have forgot us likewise.

20. He that would recommend himself to the public, let him do it by the candour and modesty of his behaviour, and by a generous indifference to external advantages. Let him love mankind, and resign to Providence, and then his works will follow him, and his good actions will praise him in the gate.

21. When you hear a discourse, let your understanding, as far as possible, keep pace with it, and lead you forward to those things which fall most within the compass of your own observations.

22. When vice and treachery shall be rewarded, and virtue and ability slighted and discountenanced; when ministers of state shall rather fear man than God, and to screen themselves run into parties and factions; when noise and clamour, and scandalous reports shall carry everything before them, it is natural to conclude that a nation in such a state of infatuation stands upon the brink of destruction, and without the intervention of some unforeseen accident, must be inevitably ruined.

23. When a prince is guarded by wise and honest men, and when all public officers are sure to be rewarded if they do well, and punished if they do evil, the consequence is plain; justice and honesty will flourish, and men will be always contriving, not for themselves, but for the honour and interest of their king and country.

24. Wicked men may sometimes go unpunished in this world, but wicked nations never do; because this world is the only place of punishment of wicked nations, though not for private and particular persons.

25. An administration that is merely founded upon human policy must be always subject to human chance; but that which is founded on the divine wisdom can no more miscarry than the government of heaven. To govern by parties and factions is the advice of an atheist, and sets up a government by the spirit of Satan. In such a government the prince can never be secure under the greatest promises, since, as men's interest changes, so will their duty and affections likewise.

26. It is a very ancient observation, and a very true one, that people generally despise where they flatter, and cringe to those they design to betray; so that truth and ceremony are, and always will be, two distinct things.

27. When you find your friend in an error, undeceive him with secrecy and civility, and let him see his oversight first by hints and glances; and if you

cannot convince him, leave him with respect, and lay the fault upon your own management.

28. When you are under the greatest vexations, then consider that human life lasts but for a moment; and do not forget but that you are like the rest of the world, and faulty yourself in many instances; and withal, remember that anger and impatience often prove more mischievous than the provocation.

29. Gentleness and good humour are invincible, provided they are without hypocrisy and design; they disarm the most barbarous and savage tempers, and make even malice ashamed of itself.

30. In all the actions of life let it be your first and principal care to guard against anger on the one hand, and flattery on the other, for they are both unserviceable qualities, and do a great deal of mischief in the government of human life.

31. When a man turns knave or libertine, and gives way to fear, jealousy, and fits of the spleen; when his mind complains of his fortune, and he quits the station in which Providence has placed him, he acts perfectly counter to humanity, deserts his own nature, and, as it were, runs away from himself.

32. Be not heavy in business, disturbed in conversation, nor impertinent in your thoughts. Let your judgment be right, your actions friendly, and your mind contented; let them curse you, threaten you, or despise you; let them go on; they can never injure your reason or your virtue, and then all the rest that they can do to you signifies nothing.

33. The only pleasure of human life is doing the business of the creation; and which way is that to be compassed very easily? Most certainly by the practice of general kindness, by rejecting the importunity of our senses, by distinguishing truth from falsehood, and by contemplating the works of the Almighty.

34. Be sure to mind that which lies before you, whether it be thought, word, or action; and never postpone an opportunity, or make virtue wait for you till to-morrow.

35. Whatever tends neither to the improvement of your reason nor the benefit of society, think it below you; and when you have done any considerable service to mankind, do not lessen it by your folly in gaping after reputation and requital.

36. When you find yourself sleepy in a morning, rouse yourself, and consider that you are born to business, and that in doing good in your generation, you answer your character and act like a man; whereas sleep and idleness do but degrade you, and sink you down to a brute.

37. A mind that has nothing of hope, or fear, or aversion, or desire, to weaken and disturb it, is the most impregnable security. Hither we may with safety retire and defy our enemies; and he that sees not this advantage must be extremely ignorant, and he that forgets it unhappy.

38. Do not disturb yourself about the faults of other people, but let everybody's crimes be at their own door. Have always this great maxim in your remembrance, that to play the knave is to rebel against religion; all sorts of injustice being no less than high treason against Heaven itself.

39. Do not contemn death, but meet it with a decent and religious fortitude, and look upon it as one of those things which Providence has ordered. If you want a cordial to make the apprehensions of dying go down a little the more easily, consider what sort of world and what sort of company you will part with. To conclude, do but look seriously into the world, and there you will see multitudes of people preparing for funerals, and mourning for their friends and acquaintances; and look out again a little afterwards, and you will see others doing the very same thing for them.

40. In short, men are but poor transitory things. To-day they are busy and harassed with the affairs of human life; and to-morrow life itself is taken from them, and they are returned to their original dust and ashes.

PART III

Containing prophetic observations relating to the affairs of Europe and of Great Britain, more particularly from 1720 to 1729.

1. In the latter end of 1720, an eminent old lady shall bring forth five sons at a birth; the youngest shall live and grow up to maturity, but the four eldest shall either die in the nursery, or be all carried off by one sudden and unexpected accident.

2. About this time a man with a double head shall arrive in Britain from the south. One of these heads shall deliver messages of great importance to the governing party, and the other to the party that is opposite to them. The first shall believe the monster, but the last shall discover the impostor, and so happily disengage themselves from a snare that was laid to destroy them and their posterity. After this the two heads shall unite, and the monster shall appear in his proper shape.

3. In the year 1721, a philosopher from Lower Germany shall come, first to Amsterdam in Holland, and afterwards to London. He will bring with him a world of curiosities, and among them a pretended secret for the transmutation of metals. Under the umbrage of this mighty secret he shall pass upon the world for some time; but at length he shall be detected, and proved to be nothing but an empiric and a cheat, and so forced to sneak off, and leave the people he has deluded, either to bemoan their loss, or laugh at their own folly. N.B.--This will be the last of his sect that will ever venture in this part of the world upon the same errand.

4. In this year great endeavours will be used for procuring a general peace, which shall be so near a conclusion that public rejoicings shall be made at the courts of several great potentates upon that account; but just in the critical juncture, a certain neighbouring prince shall come to a violent death, which shall

occasion new war and commotion all over Europe; but these shall continue but for a short time, and at last terminate in the utter destruction of the first aggressors.

5. Towards the close of this year of mysteries, a person that was born blind shall have his sight restored, and shall see ravens perch upon the heads of traitors, among which the head of a notorious prelate shall stand upon the highest pole.

6. In the year 1722, there shall be a grand congress, and new overtures of peace offered by most of the principal parties concerned in the war, which shall have so good effect that a cessation of arms shall be agreed upon for six months, which shall be kept inviolable till a certain general, either through treachery or inadvertency, shall begin hostilities before the expiration of the term; upon which the injured prince shall draw his sword, and throw the scabbard into the sea, vowing never to return it till he shall obtain satisfaction for himself, and done justice to all that were oppressed.

7. At the close of this year, a famous bridge shall be broken down, and the water that runs under it shall be tinctured with the blood of two notorious malefactors, whose unexpected death shall make mighty alterations in the present state of affairs, and put a stop to the ruin of a nation, which must otherwise have been unavoidable.

8. 1723 begins with plots, conspiracies, and intestine commotions in several countries; nor shall Great Britain itself be free from the calamity. These shall continue till a certain young prince shall take the reins of government into his own hands; and after that, a marriage shall be proposed, and an alliance concluded between two great potentates, who shall join their forces, and endeavour, in good earnest, to set all matters upon a right foundation.

9. This year several cardinals and prelates shall be publicly censured for heretical principles, and shall narrowly escape from being torn to pieces by the common people, who still look upon them as the grand disturbers of public tranquillity, perfect incendiaries, and the chief promoters of their former, present, and future calamities.

10. In 1724-5 there will be many treaties and negociations, and Great Britain, particularly, will be crowded with foreign ministers and ambassadors from remote princes and states. Trade and commerce will begin to flourish and revive, and everything will have a comfortable prospect, until some desperadoes, assisted by a monster with many heads, shall start new difficulties, and put the world again into a flame; but these shall be but of short duration.

11. Before the expiration of 1725, an eagle from the north shall fly directly to the south, and perch upon the palace of a prince, and first unravel the bloody projects and designs of a wicked set of people, and then publicly discover the murder of a great king, and the intended assassination of another greater than he.

12. In 1726, three princes will be born that will grow up to be men, and inherit the crowns of three of the greatest monarchies in Europe.

13. About this time the pope will die, and after a great many intrigues and struggles, a Spanish cardinal shall be elected, who shall decline the dignity, and declare his marriage with a great lady, heiress of one of the chief principalities in Italy, which may occasion new troubles in Europe, if not timely prevented.

14. In 1727, new troubles shall break out in the north, occasioned by the sudden death of a certain prince, and the avarice and ambition of another. Poor Poland seems to be pointed at; but the princes of the south shall enter into a confederacy to preserve her, and shall at length restore her peace, and prevent the perpetual ruin of her constitution.

15. Great endeavours will be used about this time for a comprehension in religion, supported by crafty and designing men, and a party of mistaken zealots, which they shall artfully draw in to join with them; but as the project is ill-concerted, and will be worse managed, it will come to nothing; and soon afterwards an effectual mode will be taken to prevent the like attempt for the future.

16. 1728 will be a year of inquiry and retrospection. Many exorbitant grants will be reassumed, and several persons who thought themselves secure will be called before the senate, and compelled to disgorge what they have unjustly pillaged either from the crown or the public.

17. About this time a new scaffold will be erected upon the confines of a certain great city, where an old count of a new extraction, that has been of all parties and true to none, will be doomed by his peers to make his first appearance. After this an old lady who has often been exposed to danger and disgrace, and sometimes brought to the very brink of destruction, will be brought to bed of three daughters at once, which they shall call Plenty, Peace, and Union; and these three shall live and grow up together, be the glory of their mother, and the comfort of posterity for many generations.

This is the substance of what he either writ or extracted from his papers in the interval between the loss of his speech and the return of his fit, which happened exactly at the time he had computed.

Upon the approach of his fit, he made signs to be put to bed, which was no sooner done but he was seized with extreme agonies, which he bore up under with the greatest steadfastness, and after a severe conflict, that lasted near eight hours, he expired.

Thus lived and thus died this extraordinary person; a person, though of mean extraction and obscure life, yet when his character comes to be fully and truly known, it will be read with pleasure, profit, and admiration.

His perfections at large would be the work of a volume, and inconsistent with the intention of these papers. I will, therefore, only add, for a conclusion, that he was a man of uncommon thought and judgment, and always kept his appetites and inclinations within their just limits.

His reason was strong and manly, his understanding sound and active, and his temper so easy, equal, and complaisant, that he never fell out, either with men or accidents. He bore all things with the highest affability, and computed justly upon their value and consequence, and then applied them to their proper uses.

A LETTER FROM OXFORD

Sir,

Being informed that you speedily intend to publish some memoirs relating to our dumb countryman, Dickory Cronke, I send you herewith a few lines, in the nature of an elegy, which I leave you to dispose of as you think fit. I knew and admired the man; and if I were capable, his character should be the first thing I would attempt.

Yours. &c.

AN ELEGY, IN MEMORY OF DICKORY CRONKE, THE DUMB PHILOSOPHER.

Vitiis nemo sine nascitur; optimus ille est,
Qui minimus urgetur. HORACE.

If virtuous actions emulation raise,
Then this good man deserves immortal praise.
When nature such extensive wisdom lent,
She sure designed him for our precedent.
Such great endowments in a man unknown,
Declare the blessings were not all his own;
But rather granted for a time to show
What the wise hand of Providence can do.
In him we may a bright example see
Of nature, justice, and morality;
A mind not subject to the frowns of fate,
But calm and easy in a servile state.
He always kept a guard upon his will
And feared no harm because he knew no ill.
A decent posture and an humble mien,
In every action of his life were seen.
Through all the different stages that he went,
He still appeared both wise and diligent:
Firm to his word, and punctual to his trust,
Sagacious, frugal, arable, and just.
No gainful views his bounded hopes could sway,
No wanton thought led his chaste soul astray.
In short, his thoughts and actions both declare,
Nature designed him her philosopher;
That all mankind, by his example taught,
Might learn to live, and manage every thought.

Oh! could my muse the wondrous subject grace,
And, from his youth, his virtuous actions trace;
Could I in just and equal numbers tell
How well he lived, and how devoutly fell,
I boldly might your strict attention claim,
And bid you learn, and copy out the man.

J. P.

Exeter College, August 25th, 1719.

EPITAPH

The occasion of this epitaph was briefly thus:- A gentleman, who had heard
much in commendation of this dumb man, going accidentally to the churchyard
where he was buried, and finding his grave without a tombstone, or any manner
of memorandum of his death, he pulled out his pencil, and writ as follows:

PAUPER UBIQUE JACET.

Near to this lonely unfrequented place,
Mixed with the common dust, neglected lies
The man that every muse should strive to grace,
And all the world should for his virtue prize.
Stop, gentle passenger, and drop a tear,
Truth, justice, wisdom, all lie buried here.

What, though he wants a monumental stone,
The common pomp of every fool or knave,
Those virtues which through all his actions shone
Proclaim his worth, and praise him in the grave.
His merits will a bright example give,
Which shall both time and envy too outlive.

Oh, had I power but equal to my mind,
A decent tomb should soon this place adorn,
With this inscription: Lo, here lies confined
A wondrous man, although obscurely born;
A man, though dumb, yet he was nature's care,
Who marked him out her own philosopher.

www.ingramcontent.com/pod-product-compliance
Lightning Source LLC
Chambersburg PA
CBHW071352130626
46556CB00005B/2145